In Plain Sight

Quilted Hills, Volume 1

Piper Forrest and Lily Simmons

Published by Bev Haynes, 2018.

IN PLAIN SIGHT

First edition. December 12, 2018.

ISBN: 979-8201251949

Written by Piper Forrest and Lily Simmons.

Table of Contents

Chapter 1

Abarn stood on the hill overlooking the open yard between it and the three-story house. A good size garden spread out to the left of the back porch. The whole place reflected peace and welcome. Carly passed this house many times and always felt a warming love coming from it. She remembered the sign by the road that said they took in English boarder's and called right away. She felt this place could help heal her.

The engine went silent as she pulled into a parking spot and Carly sat back in her seat finally letting go of the ignition. Above her, the walnut tree limbs spread out casting everything into a soft cooling shade. She took a deep breath before undoing the seat belt, all the while taking in her surroundings.

Carly snapped herself out of the daydreaming and wondered where she would go to let them know she arrived. "You'll never know sitting in the car."

She took a deep breath and made herself get out of the car taking only her keys. "Two weeks should do the trick." Just saying it out loud made her realize she was looking forward to staying here.

"What in the world...?"

Ruby Troyer swiped her cotton-covered arm across her sweaty brow. A river of moisture poured from under her *kapp*, a real indication her temper was becoming out of hand. She glared at the for-sale sign sitting at an angle in front of her store. She'd been pushing and pulling it for the past fifteen minutes. The post was looser now, and she scowled at the offending sign before turning her back on it. With all her might she hauled off giving a backward kick like a donkey and knocked the post and its attached sign to the ground.

It took a lot to get her temper to flare, but this was the final straw. She offered to buy the small portion of land where The Amish Country Store sat, but her neighbor, David Fisher would have none of it. He refused to sell it to her.

The property the Fisher's purchased a few months ago was the original small farm where her grandparents lived. After their grandmother died, brother Isaac sold it and moved his family to Ohio. He put the farm with a realtor, but with its small size, no one wanted it because they couldn't make a living on it. When their neighbor passed away, his widow sold her adjoining acres to David Fisher creating a large farm for his family. One of the largest in the area.

Upon a survey, Mr. Fisher found Ruby's store sat on his property, and he was determined that Ruby should move her store off his land.

Ruby's Farm Stay was very close to the Fisher property. She turned toward the *haus*, she should haul the sign to the barn. She swiped her sleeve across her brow to remove the dampness from her forehead.

Carly found herself rooted to the spot as she watched an Amish lady battle a for-sale sign. She smiled when it hit the dirt with the help of a butt smack against the post.

She giggled over her wonder with the woman, she never pictured an Amish lady to be so physical and look so satisfied by her act.

Carly wanted to meet the lady and started walking down the drive to the tidy building by the main road. She didn't want to startle the woman, so Carly cleared her throat to bring attention to her presence. "Hi, I am Carly Laine."

Carly refused to laugh when the woman jumped at her voice.

"Oh *jah*, the *Englisch* woman that wants to stay for two weeks."

Carly saw the high color in the woman's cheeks and wished she knew why she attacked the sign. When the lady went to lift the offensive thing, Carly leaned down and helped to stand it upright.

"Miss Laine, shall we carry this up to the *haus*?"

"Sounds good to me."

Together they made their way to a side door Carly failed to see before. Once they reached the house, they braced the sign up against the outside wall. "Looks good."

"*Jah*, I am Ruby Troyer." She held out her hand for Miss Laine to take. "We will take a drink."

"I would like that. Please call me Carly."

Ruby smiled at the woman, "not the proper way, but then you are an *Englisch* woman, Carly. Ruby is good between us."

Carly smiled back at Ruby, "I understand." In other's presence, she would call her Mrs. Troyer. Such formality was foreign in her own life.

"Come in, come into my kitchen." Ruby stepped aside then smiled at her new customer. "I will call my son Matthew to come and take your luggage up to your room." Ruby took her cell phone from her apron pocket and sent a quick text to her son.

Now that her anger, not becoming to the Amish, faded her legs went shaky. *Nee*, she couldn't give in to the weakness. She needed to remain strong in the Amish community. Tonight, she would pray for forgiveness for her anger. Guilt surged through her. She had to forgive David Fisher for his stubbornness. *Be kind to one another, tender-hearted, forgiving each other, just as God in Christ also has forgiven you.*

She couldn't help but see her customer's eyebrows raise as she tucked the phone back into her apron. *Jah*, it was unusual for the Amish to use electricity and telephones. It had taken her a long time to gain permission from the Bishop to allow this. She and the farm were a substantial donor to the health fund for her Amish community. She could only use her cell phone for emergencies and for her business. It angered many in the community, but she was not concerned because this was her business and not theirs.

Miss Carly Laine. Ruby couldn't help but look at her again. She was attractive for an *Englischer*, Ruby liked her short haircut and the bouncy curls of blonde hair, she held a manner about herself that made a person feel fresh and free in her company. The row of freckles across her nose with those full pink lips looked impish like in a child's book. Miss Laine would be the only guest booked for two weeks, which was quite unusual, but the busy time would come later as summer came upon them. The *Englisch* schools were in session until mid-June. After that time, the farm would be hopping as her son was fond of saying.

Thinking of Matthew brought a smile to her face and calmed her heart. The boy, or she should say, young *mann*, was now eighteen. She still thought of him as her baby, maybe all *maem's* did. He did not appreciate her coddling. After all, he was courting Hannah Fisher, the girl from next door. Dear, sweet Hannah. She helped Ruby at the house. Cleaning rooms and washing. It was too bad her father was such a problem. He was the miserable *mann* to put the for-sale sign in front of her store.

Ruby moved about the large kitchen. She gathered drinking glasses and a pitcher of meadow tea for them to drink and placed them at one end of the long table.

"My son will be here in a blink, he is just at the barn."

"I love this kitchen, Ruby, it's so huge."

"We never know how many will take dinner with us."

Carly smiled, then asked, "How many people can sit around this table?"

"Many. Twenty if all the leaves are in it." Ruby smiled back at her guest. "Come sit and rest a bit."

"I'm fine but definitely thirsty."

They both sat with the cool glasses of tea. The back door leading into the mudroom slammed with a bang. Matthew rushed into the kitchen. "*Maem*," he nodded, then looked at the guest. "To which room should I take her luggage?"

"The big master at the back," Ruby looked at Carly and tipped her head, "You look like you could use a good bit of rest."

Matthew walked around the table, and turned toward his *maem* asking, "is Hannah somewhere in the *haus* working?"

Ruby shook her head. "*Nee*, I haven't seen her today. She would normally be here for a couple of hours."

Matthews brows knit together. "Oh no, her father said she didn't come down to fix breakfast this morning either. When he went to her room, her bed was already made, but she was nowhere to be found."

"Did he check the barn?"

Matthew nodded. "He's checked everywhere, and he can't find her."

Matthew told Ruby last week that he and Hannah were courting. She was very happy for her son, and now, she understood why he was as concerned as the girl's father. "Well, when she shows up, I will let you know. Get some tea, Matthew." Ruby pointed to the pitcher. "She has to be somewhere close by. Can you think of anywhere son?"

Ruby looked at Carly as her guest took a quick breath. The girl began speaking hesitantly. "M-maybe you should call the police and get them to help find her. Waiting is never a good idea, especially if she didn't come home last night."

Ruby and Matthew exchanged looks. "I'm sorry Miss Laine, but that is not the Amish way. We deal with issues ourselves. Hannah's father will take this to the Bishop. If he feels it's necessary, the Bishop will assemble a search from the members of our community."

Carly's dark brows knit together, and a deep line creased the space between them. Taking a deep breath, she said, "I'm a private detective, and I specialize in finding people. I'll be glad to help."

Ruby spoke up before Matthew could answer. "We will take care of this in the Amish way, the men will search for Hannah. I will tell her father of your offer when next I see him." She hoped her guest understood. It was a kind thing for her to offer.

They finished their tea, Matthew picked up Carly's bags and he took her to the room. After settling in Carly said she wanted to walk about for a bit and then sit on the front porch. She told Matthew that it visually welcomed her when she arrived.

Chapter 2

Ruby opened the refrigerator door and moved around bowls covered with pretty, plastic bonnet covers. She only needed to cook for four people tonight: Matthew, her sister, Miriam, the guest Carly Laine, and herself. She had a big bowl of dressing leftover and the baked chicken from yesterday's Sunday dinner. It would be plenty good for the evening meal. She would mix it together with mushroom soup and create a casserole. This morning, she harvested a large bag of spinach, pulled up a red onion to dice into the greens, and she would add mandarin oranges and a sweet dressing. A peach pie topped with vanilla ice cream would finish off supper.

Having the meal settled in her mind, she walked through the kitchen and into the mudroom. Turning, she entered the laundry room, a small room attached to the side of the *haus* when the farm became the business.

Doing up all the sheets and towels was a never-ending process. A gas generator powered the two washers and two dryers, and there was a long table used for folding sitting across from them. She only used the dryers on bad weather days for she liked the smell of fresh air on the sheets.

Pulling back the curtains she peered out the window. The wash from yesterday was down, so Hannah completed her chores. *Where was that girl?* By this time of the day, the towels should be neatly folded and placed on the table, and the sheets in the washers. Hannah had never been late since she started working at the Inn.

Ruby sighed deeply, then turned on her heel and headed for the upstairs rooms. Three guests checked out, and the rooms needed completion.

An hour later, Ruby put the bathroom linens in the washer and the sheets in a large basket to take to the line. She did them in reverse order because it was getting later in the day, and she wanted the sheets to dry before the sun went down.

She carefully stepped down the three wooden steps to the ground as someone took the basket from her arms. Looking up she saw David Fisher standing there with her bundle. "Oh, you frightened the life from me," Ruby uttered.

"Mrs. Troyer, are you having to do my Hannah's work today?"

Ruby couldn't tell if the *mann* was worried or angry. His face flushed red which made his bright blue eyes even more vivid. "*Jah,* but please, just call me Ruby. We are neighbors, after all."

They walked to the clothesline at the back of the *haus* without saying a word. They had a pulley system drying line with two wheels, one on the *haus* and another high on the barn. All she had to do was pin on the sheets, glide the cable away from her and add another. The line carried the wash up high off the ground as it traveled toward the other pulley on the barn. David set the basket on the table, so she could reach the sheets without bending over.

David placed his hand over Ruby's as she reached for the first sheet. "Did you tear down the for-sale sign I put in front of your store?"

Ruby looked from his hand to his face. She did not want to answer him. The anger started bubbling up within her again. Did she have no self-control? Pulling in a deep breath, she nodded.

The *mann* removed his hand from hers and jammed his fists on his hips. "I have had enough of your antics, woman. I was trying to help you. If someone bought the building to haul away, it would serve both of us." His face reddened, and a wild gleam flashed from his gaze. "You have six weeks left to move that building from my land. If you choose not to," he leaned toward her, "I will hire a bulldozer to level it. Do you understand me?"

Ruby knew he was serious. She also knew that she had little choice in the matter, but it made her spitting mad. If he came to her politely and told her about the discrepancy in the land survey, she would have found some way to work with him, but no, he had stormed to her door in a rage, making demands. The only thing his attitude accomplished was to jump on her last nerve and off went her anger as well.

"Mr. Fisher, your demands are getting you nowhere with me. How can we move a building that's nearly one hundred years old? It will fall apart. I would buy the bit of land it sits on if you would be reasonable, but *nee*, you want to holler and snort like a raging bull. Refusing to sell it is not helping either one of us."

"Your stubborn attitude is not helping either," he said and began pacing back and forth by the pole holding up her washing line.

Suddenly, all the air seemed to rush from him, and he dropped into a squat. He pulled his light-colored straw hat from his head then ran his fingers through his blond hair. If Ruby had not been so angry with him, she could feel sad for him.

"Mr. Fisher are you ok?"

"I am sorry, Ruby. I came here to talk to you about Hannah, not harass you about the store building." He stood, still holding his hat in his hand. "I am so worried about my girl."

Tears pooled in his eyes, and Ruby's anger fled so swiftly from her, it made her knees go weak. "Oh, Mr. Fisher, please know that I'd do anything to help find Hannah."

David leaned against the pole holding the line. "I spoke to Bishop Yoder. He's assembling a search party to look for Hannah."

"When was the last time anyone saw her?"

"Last night at the end of the singing. She and her friend, Mary Eischler, were together. When your son came out to bring Hannah home, she was not there."

Ruby shook her head. Where could the girl have gone? "Matthew is concerned. I saw how broken-hearted he became when I told him she was not at work today."

Moving from his stance against the pole, David put his hat back on his head.

"Before you go, would you be interested in talking to someone that may be able to help in locating Hannah?"

David's blonde brows knit together, and he tipped his head in question. "I do not understand."

"It is not really the Amish way, but I have a guest here at the farm stay who is a person that locates missing people. She has some ideas she offered when Matthew came in to attend to her luggage. He told me about Hannah disappearing. She might give us some ideas to find your daughter."

The *mann* stood looking at her. Ruby felt his uncertainty. He slowly nodded. "It could not hurt to hear different ideas. Of course, we'll keep this between us, *Jah?*"

"*Jah.* For sure and certain. The Bishop would have us in front of the church members asking for our forgiveness if he knew we were involving the *Englisch*. She is Carly Laine, and she is sitting up on the front porch."

David nodded at Ruby, "I will go see the lady and see if she can help."

He waved back at Ruby as he walked toward the porch.

Chapter 3

David left Ruby Troyer's farm stay and ambled over to his place. He had spoken for a few minutes with her guest, but he felt nervous about it and couldn't concentrate. All her thoughts were so negative. He wanted to stay positive. He knew Hannah would be home soon. At least he prayed she would.

He should not have verbally assaulted Ruby as he did. She was innocent in the survey discrepancy. What would he do if he were her? The store was part of her business.

He yawned as he stood looking at the three short steps leading into his mud room. All night he stayed awake fretting about Hannah. He expected her to come in at any time. He thought she was with her beau, Matthew, but knowing the boy as he did, the later it got, he knew Matthew wouldn't keep Hannah out that late.

David sighed, then navigated the steps into the *haus*. He would stretch out on his recliner and take a nap. It would make time pass while the searchers gathered. Even thirty minutes would help.

Closing his eyes, all he could see was Martha. His wife had been with *Gott* for three years now. She had a quickly spreading brain cancer. He and the *kinner* hadn't become used to the notion that she was sick when she died. Just like that. One morning she didn't awaken. He had slept beside her as she passed, and he hadn't realized it until morning.

Martha would have been so upset at Hannah's disappearance. He wished she were here by him now. They would give each other comfort and hope. Right now, David was not optimistic.

He thought moving to Paradise Wells would solve all his problems. In Ohio, he had only a small farm. When he saw this land for-sale, he quickly sold his farm to his neighbor giving the *mann* more land and snatched up this Pennsylvania property before anyone else could put in an offer.

Truth be known, everywhere he turned he saw Martha in their Ohio home, and he needed to start over.

He missed his wife, he feared for Hannah, and now there was another worry for him. His neighbor Ruby Troyer. The deep-red haired woman with the bright blue eyes made him catch his breath, and his heart start a runaway beat every time he saw her. Ruby's skin was so smooth she looked to be sixteen, but he thought she'd be close to his age of thirty-seven. His eyes opened, and he looked out the window. The trees swayed gently in his front yard,

Ruby. Why did he act so gruff when he was around her? Deep down, he knew. He felt an attraction to her, and he'd like to get to know her better. Maybe after Hannah came home.

Just as he slipped into a light sleep, he heard buggies approaching. The searchers had arrived.

Ruby stood at the kitchen sink running cold water over the hard-boiled eggs. She swirled the pot, then bounced the eggs up and down. The shells quickly fell off the whites leaving a glossy sheen in the pan. She reached into the water, fished out the eggs, and dropped them into a large bowl.

Her sister Miriam was chopping boiled potatoes for the salad. "I'm happy Matthew came for me, Ruby. We all need to help in the search for Hannah."

"*Jah,* and in our district, we've all come together to create food for all sorts of gatherings. No one duplicates as we all know what each of us brings." Ruby's tone was reflective of her thoughts. Funerals, barn raising, any number of groups, but this was the first search party she could think of. All the men in the district would be on the hunt for Hannah.

Ruby quickly chopped the eggs then covered them with a plastic bonnet top. They went into the gas-powered refrigerator to chill. The shower cap appearing protectors were reusable where plastic wrap was disposable. The sticky substance frustrated Ruby, it always ended up a wadded mess in her hands, so when she found the new coverings at the big box store near Lancaster, she purchased four boxes. They would last her a long time. The *Englisch* store was noted for discontinuing items. Usually, things Ruby loved.

"I'll chop the onions and celery if you would go downstairs to the pantry for the sweet pickle relish after you finish up the potatoes and get them cooling." Ruby tore off three celery stalks and began dicing them finely.

Within an hour the sisters had fifty sandwiches made and wrapped in waxed paper and the potato salad in a large stainless-steel bowl.

Just then, her boarder, Carly Laine entered the kitchen.

"Oh good! You're back," Ruby said, "you can help us carry the food to the Fishers. It isn't far enough to harness the horse and take the buggy. You don't mind, do you?"

"No, I will be glad to help."

"Was there any information from the police department?" Ruby asked as she rinsed her hands under the faucet then pulled a towel from her shoulder and dried them.

"Yes, I spoke to Ash Folsham, my ex-partner when I was with the department. I have a report about other missing girls at the settlement in Williamsport."

"Other girls? How many are missing?" Miriam asked.

"He isn't sure the exact number, but at least three girls are missing there. I have the names for Mr. Fisher."

"This isn't in a district close to us, Williamsport is a long way from here." She ran her hands down her apron as they became clammy with nerves. "It's *wunderbar* you were able to get this information, but Carly, I fear that bishop Yoder won't be pleased to have the police involved. We Amish take care of our own business." She feared to say this to her guest. The woman had been so kind as to help them with the information. Would the Bishop chastise her for involving Carly? "Carly, this is my sister Miriam. She lives near here, just to the north less than a mile. She runs the store for us."

"It's so nice to meet you, Miriam. Your sister has been very accommodating." Carly turned back to Ruby and said, "I understand the dynamics of this situation, and so does Detective Folsham. The one thing he feels is important is that it might be a widespread operation. Also, he thinks there is a time element."

"Time element? She's only been missing since last night. Not even twenty-four hours."

"True, but if it is organized crime then they will be delivering or moving the girls very quickly, so we don't have much time to find her."

Ruby dropped onto a wooden chair near the table. "Organized crime? Surely not! What would they want with Hannah?" She dabbed at the corner of her eyes with her dirty apron, and she sniffed the tears back not wanting to cry in front of her guest. Right now, she didn't feel so emotionally secure.

Carly took in a deep breath, knowing this would only upset Ruby even more. "Any of these girls can be missing for a specific reason...."

"Then we'd better get over to the Fisher's place with the food, so you can tell David Fisher what you've learned. The Bishop will most probably be with him." She pushed in the chair, grabbed the bowl of potato salad, and handed it to Carly.

AMISH POTATO SALAD

INGREDIENTS

3 pounds potatoes, cut into quarters

1 cup mayonnaise

½ cup sugar

2 tablespoons yellow mustard

2 tablespoons vinegar

1 teaspoons salt

4 hard boiled eggs, peeled and chopped

1 cup onions, finely chopped

DIRECTIONS

Place the potatoes in a large pot, fill with enough water to cover potatoes. Bring to a boil and cook about 20 minutes, or until fork tender. Drain, set aside to cool.

In a medium bowl combine mayo, sugar, mustard, vinegar and salt, mix well.

Place the potatoes, eggs, onion and celery in a large bowl. Pour in the dressing and gently stir until thoroughly mixed.

MEADOW TEA

1-gallon water
　　2 packed cups fresh mint, whole
1 cup sugar

DIRECTIONS

This recipe makes 1 gallon of iced tea - enough to fill an average sized "sun tea" jar.

Boil water in a large pot.

Rinse mint leaves - keep whole. I do this in a colander - inspect and rinse well - I always find lots of sticky little critters on mint.

Add mint to a pot of boiling water.

Cover pot and remove from heat and let steep for 2½ - 3 hours.

Remove whole mint leaves with a slotted spoon. Let leaves drain and dry in a colander. Leaves can be reused once for another batch of tea.

Pour tea thru a fine screen into your storage container. If you don't have a screen you could use a sifter or even a kitchen towel. Please use something - you don't want bits and pieces of leaves floating around.

Stir in sugar to taste. Suggest 1 cup per gallon.

Refrigerate, serve cold. Enjoy :)

Chapter 4

The Troyer farm was the closest to the Fisher's in their district, so Ruby, Miriam, and Carly were the first to arrive with their food contribution. Miriam shifted the salad bowl in her arms to free her hand to open the door leading to the kitchen. The women entered with a shout out to anyone that might be at home. The interior of the house was quiet, so they set about putting the food in the refrigerator until it was needed for the noon meal when the searchers would descend. Hopefully, they would bring Hannah with them.

Ruby looked around the kitchen. A new propane cooking stove and new gas refrigerator stood in place of the old appliances her brother had sold with the *haus*. The kitchen floor was new as well. She didn't know how she felt about the changes. It made her miss her grandparents even more. This had been their family home for years and years. Now, the Fisher's lived here, and she was happy to see that they made the place a home for them, but the sadness for the old folks remained.

Carly scanned the room as different ladies entered. They all looked too fresh and peaceful in their *kapps* and dresses. Only two plain women stood out. Ruby and Miriam. Both had red hair, Ruby's dark red where Miriam's was lighter but still fiery. All of them wore the starched aprons with perfect bows. She looked down at her tee-shirt and jeans and felt extremely uncomfortable. She could already imagine the Bishop's condemning glare, and he hadn't even arrived.

She found Ruby and went over to her. Carly didn't wait for the lady to figure out the problem or notice her. Her hold on Ruby's arm stayed firm, "I need to talk to you...now."

"What is the matter, Carly. You look upset?"

Carly ignored the question and pulled Ruby into the small hall off the kitchen. "Okay, I need to be more presentable than this." She pulled on her shirt and looked down, Ruby quickly picked up on the problem.

"I understand, Carly, but no one here thinks badly of you. We are used to the *Englisch* ways. It might be worse if you tried to look like us. The others might feel you are mocking us. Your clothing is fine." She smiled at Carly. "*Nee* worries coming from you. You will have your hands full enough explaining to the Bishop why you are here and have spoken to the police." She turned as another woman entered the back door with her hands full. "*Kamme,* let's help Letty with the food. See if you can shove more into the refrigerator."

Carly rushed over and took most of the dishes out of her hands. The refrigerator was packed, but she managed to get all the bowls inside. "I think that's all that will fit in here for now."

"How about you stay here and deal with the food, and I'll get a couple women to help me set up the tables. I hear some buggies coming up the drive now. We can get the food out as soon as we have a place for it."

"I will start taking them out once you let me know you're ready."

Carly stood looking in amazement as the women moved in a relay line from the house to the tables. Soon, all the food was ready for the men, and Ruby called to the men to the table, then the whole group bowed their head in silent prayer.

She waited until the prayer was finished and then rushed back into the kitchen. Carly remembered she had not seen any silverware or dishes brought out from the house. She went through every drawer and cabinet until she had everything on a large tray. It was a heavy load.

"Oh, thank you, Carly! We were so intent on the food we missed a way to eat." She laughed boisterously as they rushed out the door to save the day.

Carly spotted a man with a long white beard, and a tan woven hat watching her. She put her load at the end of the table where everyone would start.

"Bishop Yoder," Ruby called to the gentleman, "I'd like you to meet my guest, Carly Laine. She is helping us today."

Carly held out her hand. The man didn't take it, he crinkled his nose in distaste. At his hesitation, she pulled her hand back. She scolded herself, knowing it was the wrong thing to do. They both watched as he nodded to Ruby and walked to the table for his meal.

Carly whispered to Ruby, "I think I should follow him and tell him what I found out."

"*Nee!*"

Carly spun around only to see David Fisher behind her. He had his hands on the hips of his dark blue, simple pants. Suspenders hung on tightly at the waistband to keep them up. He pushed his straw summer hat back on his head, and the blonde, bowl cut hair peeked out around the edges. His face reddened with anger.

"Well, we need to talk to you then, Mr. Fisher. I've learned a lot from the police."

David grasped Carly's elbow and guided her away from the serving table. "*Do come* Miss..."

"Carly Laine," Ruby said, walking toward the *haus* with them, and reminding the *mann* of her guest's name.

Carly felt David release her arm as soon as she quit pulling away from him. She walked up the steps to the mudroom and followed the man and woman inside. They walked toward the large family table in the middle of the kitchen, and each took a seat. The women sat across from David Fisher.

Carly pulled the list from her jeans pocket and unfolded it. "My ex-partner at the station gave this to me." She passed David the list of missing girls from a district up north. "He said that none of the girls have been found..." Carly hesitated, and Ruby practically nudged her on. "He also said that he believes it is organized crime." That instantly brought the man's attention to Carly.

"You are telling me that my daughter has been taken to sell?"

She'd been mistaken, it appeared Mr. Fisher had already thought of the possibility. "I am sorry to say that it is possible. I'm surprised you know of such things."

"The Amish are not idiots, Miss Laine. Because we are not part of the *Englisch* world does not mean we are ignorant of its workings."

Ruby saw large tears form in the crystal blue of David Fishers' eyes. She looked away to give the man his dignity. Seeing him upset caused tears in her own eyes as well, and she swallowed hard to keep them from spilling over her lashes. Her crying would help no one as she watched Carly wiping away her tears.

A commotion outside drew their attention. David stood and walked outside. "Ruben Eischler is here, and he looks mighty upset." With that, David rushed down the three steps and out toward the *mann* and his horse and buggy.

Ruby grabbed Carly's hand and pulled her through the kitchen and mudroom. "What's going on, Ruby?"

"I do not know, but we need to find out. Remember, please stay near the women. I'll verge as close as I can to the men. They will not think anything of it, but if you are near, they will back away." They walked out to the tables of food underneath the giant trees.

Ruby stood near the garden and could hear Mr. Eischler in his agitated state.

"When she didn't come down after breakfast, the Missus went up and found her bed had not been slept in."

David spoke up, "You are saying that your Mary is missing too?"

"*Jah!*"

After hearing the news, the bishop walked toward the group of men finishing their meal and told them of Mary Eischler's disappearance as well as Hannah Fisher. Then he called for a silent prayer.

Once he looked up to end the prayer, he walked away from them, his long legs carrying him toward David Fisher. "You should tell us what the outsider has brought for information."

David nodded, then walked toward the gathering of searchers. "Ruby Troyer's guest is a private detective from Lancaster. She will tell you what she's found out." David looked at Carly.

She hesitated a second before stepping toward the group, thankfully Ruby stayed beside her or Carly might have collapsed. Knowing what she needed to tell them, it wouldn't be easy, but as David said they are not ignorant.

"Mr. Fisher has a list of other Amish girls that have gone missing over the last few months. I spoke to my ex-partner at the station in Lancaster, and the consensus is that these girls were taken by organized crime."

All the men broke out to talk to each other. Carly stared at the Bishop. He was watching her and nodded in silence to her. Carly moved away with Ruby when the lady took her hand, but then Carly remembered something and stopped. "Mr. Fisher? Did you get a chance to speak to the teacher?"

David raised his hand to silence the men, "*Nee*, Mr. Thomas Glick was not available."

Carly grabbed her bottom lip with her teeth, worrisome habit she always carried.

The Bishop stepped forward, and all attention went to him. "Mr. Glick is not of this district but Williamsport, he is here only until Mary can take over the teaching position permanently."

Matthew, Ruby's son, pushed through the crowd to stand in front of the Bishop. Carly gripped Ruby's wrist to stop her from going to him. She whispered, "he needs to do this Ruby."

Ruby nodded to her, and they both stayed silent; Carly could see the anger building in the young man.

"Bishop Yoder, we should allow the police to help us." Matthew took in a deep breath, "None of us are capable of handling organized crime and their intent."

Ruby saw the Bishop nod as he took in Matthew's angst. She swallowed hard fearing what the *mann* would tell her son. She turned her head to look at the Bishop. All eyes were on the man awaiting his verdict in the matter.

Slowly, the Bishop nodded. "*Jah,* we have had no success in our search. Ruben and David, please go into town and speak to the police about our missing girls. Miss Laine, will you kindly accompany them? You know more about their procedures and all three of you can report back to us."

Carly reached out and took hold of Ruby's arm, "Please come with me."

Ruby looked over her shoulder to the bishop. He nodded his approval, but his face was still scowling.

Chapter 5

As they backed out from Ruby's drive, Carly looked in her rearview mirror and saw the men starting out in the buggy. She could see Matthew joined the fathers as well as bishop Yoder and wondered if Ruby knew.

Ruby seemed to be checking out the inside of her car. "Do you ride in cars?" Carly asked her.

"*Jah,* we do. We hire a driver when we go long distances. It isn't safe for the horses as they tire easily." She turned around and peered out the back window. "Matthew came with? And the Bishop, too?" She asked, turning to Carly.

"Yes, I saw them get into the wagon. Will anyone bother your farm or house while we're away?"

With a deep sigh, Ruby said, "Thank you for worrying, but my sister Miriam, went back to the store following lunch. She'll see anyone drive in or any deliveries."

"That is good to know. It is going to take a while for Ash Folsham to take down all the information from the fathers, and you and Matthew." Carly worried her lip again and knew it would be sore by tonight. She decided to ask Ruby about the teacher. "Ruby, do you know the teacher, Mr. Glick, very well?"

"*Nee...*" She scratched at a spot on her apron. "Only that he came from Williamsport to fill in while the board came up with a teacher from within our district. It is the way we fill the position." She looked up with tears in her eyes. "Mary is to take over the teaching in the fall when school starts up again."

"So, this Mr. Glick has been here awhile?"

"Why do you want to know all this? Surely, it isn't important to find the girls."

Carly wondered if she should tell Ruby what she thought and decided the lady needed to know. "Ruby, the Bishop said that the man came from Williamsport."

"*Jah,* so why is this important?"

"Because Ruby, that is where the other Amish girls are missing from." She took a deep breath over her reaction to the fact. "I am just curious because of the connection. Maybe Ash can check him out."

Shaking her head, Ruby said, "I cannot believe anyone in our community would do something like this. There is no reason behind it. Thomas Glick is well liked and helps us all where he can. He was at the last barn raising. You know, I think he is a cousin to Bishop Yoder."

"That is probably all we have, but let's have Ash run a check just to satisfy my curiosity."

Their conversation ended as they started to enter the city and Carly needed to put her attention on the traffic.

Once in town Carly watched for a side street, she knew that would take them away from the main road and all the tourist traffic. She loved the area around here with the quaint shops and even the buggies that slowed traffic to a crawl. "Oh look, is that Mr. Fisher's wagon? He must have come in another way."

"For sure and certain. There is a lane from our farm to Lancaster that is only five miles in distance. The highway takes twenty miles."

"Really?" Carly didn't bother hiding her annoyance. "Maybe we can take it home." She almost laughed but managed to swallow it. "We are here."

She pulled the car into an open space just as the men got out of the buggy and tied it off to the hitching post.

Carly closed Ash's office door and joined the group waiting for her. "He will be right with us, he needs to make sure we will have a room." She remembered to mention to Ash to ask about any strangers or delivery trucks that might have shown up around the community. Carly thought of asking them but thought better of it. Ash needed to be there to hear their answers.

She saw him coming up to them and smiled.

"Everyone, this is Mr. Ash Folsham, he will be the detective handling the case of your daughters. Detective Folsham, this is Bishop Yoder, Mr. David Fisher is Hannah's father, and Ruben Eischler is Mary's father." She felt the tension in the room. None of them shook Ash's hand nor looked him in the eyes. She did catch the glower on Matthew's face, and realized she left him out. "Matthew Troyer is Hannah's intended and Ruby's son."

The bishop's head jerked in Matthew's direction. "What? You are courting Hannah?'

Matthew nodded. "We only told my mother and her father. We hadn't had time to contact you about it, Bishop Yoder."

Ruby offered her hand to the detective. "I'm Ruby Troyer, and Matthew is my son. Hannah works at my farm stay."

The bishop looked angry, his face pulled into a deeper scowl than she had seen earlier. Carly wasn't sure if that anger was aimed at Matthew or his mother.

The red-faced Bishop lost control. "Your independent nature will bring you nothing but trouble, Matthew. We will talk about this later. I will come to your home when we arrive to speak to both you and your mother. I have concerns about the farm as well."

Carly sucked in her breath causing Ash to turn to her. She shook her head to stop him from saying anything, the Bishop was angry enough.

Ash acknowledged the lady, "Please, could you all follow me. We will record our conversation, it will make it easier than taking individual statements."

Everyone proceeded into the room and took a seat. Carly found it interesting that Ruby followed David to the other side of the long table and sat between him and her son. The bishop still looked ticked off, and Carly didn't think he would cool down anytime soon.

"Miss Laine. You should ask the questions as you are familiar with the case." Ash never looked up from shuffling his papers.

Carly swallowed her surprise and decided, why not. "That is fine, detective." she caught his smile even though he still didn't raise his head. "I think we should start with Hannah's father as she was the first that we knew was missing. Could you explain the events of yesterday, Mr. Fisher?"

He proceeded to give his version of discovering his daughter's failure to come home the night before. Carly listened to everything, but nothing came up that was different than she knew. Once Mr. Fisher was finished, she asked Matthew to tell them his discovery.

Again, nothing new came forward from Matthew. She turned her attention to Mary's father. She wished his wife could have been here, but that wouldn't have happened. It seemed Mr. Eischler was very staunch like the Bishop and would never have allowed it. Yet, she could hear how upset he was over his daughter, he loved her very much. When he finished, Carly put her attention on the bishop. "Bishop Yoder, you organized the search of the community and nearby woods, did anyone find any item or evidence of the girls?"

It seemed to take the man too long to address her question. She swore if he made any nasty remarks about her being involved, she'd let her temper rain all over him.

"*Nee*, we found nothing, not even evidence of a struggle. Whoever took them had to have done it closer to the barn."

"Did you and the men search that area?" Carly felt the man hesitated to answer.

"I checked that area and the surrounding buildings and found nothing."

"It seems the girls vanished." Ash's statement drew everyone's attention. "From what you have all stated there was no reason the girls would leave on their own. No, there is evidence, we just haven't found it. I would like to come out there with my forensic team and see if we can find anything."

Immediately, the men started speaking. Ash held up his hand to quiet the room, "I understand this goes against the rules for your community, but the longer these girls are missing, the less chance we have to find them."

Bishop Yoder spoke up, "this goes against our laws, and you very well know it."

Ash nodded at the man, "Yes. I know this, but I would think that an exception could be made."

It was Hannah's father, David Fisher that stood up and faced the Bishop. "You and your team are welcome to come to my place..." he paused and looked at Mary's father who nodded yes to David. "Mary's father agrees as well. We will also ask our neighbors for permission for you to search the fields and woods."

Carly noticed that David refused to look at the Bishop and she could see how angry both fathers were over his refusal to grant an exception.

Ash nodded and said they would be out there within an hour. He then called an end to the meeting.

Chapter 6

Ruby paced across the kitchen. First, wiping the table for the sixth time then making *kaffe,* and looking at the whoopie pies in her pantry. Everything was ready for when Bishop Yoder came to call.

All Ruby could think about was how she extended her hand to the detective as an introduction at the police building. She knew this was too forward and definitely un-Amish. Had running her business made her too *Englisch*? She hadn't thought so, but now looking back, her manner surely wasn't Old Order Amish. She could be in so much trouble with the bishop.

Matthew was another matter entirely. Why was the bishop angry with her son? Surely, his courting Hannah would not upset the *mann*. At some point, the couple would have to meet with the leader, but not until they decided to marry.

Both her son, and Hannah were baptized, and free to marry at any time. Still, she couldn't get the stern, angry look off Bishop Yoder's face from her mind. He was a staunch old *mann* and ruled the district with his iron hand, but only because it followed the Bible teachings and their *Ordnung.*

The sound of horseshoes on her gravel drive made her stomach flip. The Bishop was here. She'd better call Matthew who was working in the barn. She took her phone out and quickly texted her son. The knock at the door came as she slipped her phone into her dress pocket under her apron.

Ruby walked through the living room and stood in front of the door. She tucked her hair into her bonnet making sure no stray hairs had come loose. Opening the door, she pasted on a fake smile. Ruby prayed the bishop wouldn't notice that she was nervous to see him.

"*Willkom*, Bishop."

The *mann* walked into the room without a greeting in return. "Where is Matthew?"

"He will be here in a bit. I just told him you were arriving." Ruby felt her face flush with heat. She should not have said that. The bishop might question her use of the cell phone. Many business owners in their district used the cell phone, but they were men. She had to fight for everything she had at the farm, and she always felt she was on thin ice where the church was concerned. Or should she say, Bishop Yoder? The *mann* terrified her.

"Would you like a cup of *kaffe*? I have moon pies to go with it."

"Fine." Bishop Yoder walked into the kitchen and made himself at home at the large table. He looked around the room.

Ruby poured the *kaffe* and set it in front of him then went for the moon pies in the pantry. "Do you need cream and sugar, Bishop?"

"*Nee*, black is fine for me."

She took the dish towel off the treats and set them on the table. Sitting across from the *mann*, she watched him intently as he took a napkin from the holder at the middle of the table, then placed the treat on it. Why didn't she put a paper plate out for him? Oh, *Jah*...she remembered. She didn't want him chastising her for the modern ways of paper. It was *Englisch*.

After the *mann* sipped his steaming *kaffe* in complete silence, he looked up as Matthew entered through the back door. The mud room was at the back, so any work clothing and muddy boots could be removed to keep the interior of the *haus* as clean as possible. There were many "leavings" in the barn area that were not appreciated in the house.

"*Maem*, Bishop Yoder..." Matthew said. He took a cup from a hook under the cabinet and poured himself a cup of *kaffe* and walked to the table.

He sat beside her. Just having him near made Ruby relax. The boy might only be eighteen, but he was a *mann* at that age, having been on his own without his father since age twelve. It made him grow up quickly.

"I'll start out our conversation, bishop, by asking what the purpose of your call is? I picked up on the feeling today that you were unhappy with *maem* and me today." Matthew snatched a napkin and put two pies on it.

The Bishop's face reddened behind his white beard and white chopped, bowl cut hair. His watery, faded blue eyes snapped in anger. "You are very perceptive, Matthew. First, I want to say I'm disappointed that you and Hannah didn't tell me that you had started courting."

Matthew nodded. "And? That you said "first" says that there is more you want to discuss."

"*Wonnernaus!*"

"None of my business? Everything between *maem* and the farm is my business. You see, *maem* put it all in my name. The Troyer Farm Stay is mine, and anything about it pertains to me."

Ruby thought the bishop would faint on the spot. For as red as his face had been it now was as white as his whiskers. She felt laughter play against her tummy, but she swallowed to keep it down. This was no time to laugh. Just realizing that the bishop knew he couldn't antagonize her anymore was a delight. Oh, how proud she was of Matthew as he sat there facing down the leader of their *Ordnung*.

Bishop Yoder slammed his fist down on the table making the center items of napkins, and salt and pepper shakers jump and fall over.

"Oh!" Ruby cried. She didn't know how to react.

"Then you better have a word with your mother about her actions and the people she brings to this... *haus*." He looked around in distaste. "This place does not look Amish. You put in pamphlets that it is an Amish experience. To me, it looks *Englisch*. You act *Englisch* woman. If you do not want to enter the shunning, you had better change your ways."

Ruby didn't know how to react. *Shunning?* "Bishop, I have done nothing wrong to deserve shunning. I suspect I am the largest contributor to the general fund to help with other's medical bills, help rebuild barns and for the good of our district. I am not saying this with pride. It is a statement only."

"*Jah!* But that does not mean we have not seen you change. Look at what you did today. You brought that *Englisch* policewoman upon us. It is none of her business how we search for our girls. Now, the entire police department of Lancaster is involved."

Matthew stood, slammed his hands on his hips and said, his voice rising with each word, "I *want* the police involved. I want Hannah and Mary back. The sooner that happens, the happier I will be."

"You dare speak to me that way Matthew? I could ask the members for a vote on your shunning as well."

Shaking his head, Matthew responded, "I didn't mean to get carried away, but I'm upset and tired. I can hardly think of another night that Hannah and Mary are alone and in the dark. If you must shun us, then well enough, but it won't keep me from searching for our women, and it won't keep us from running our business."

The bishop stood. "I see nothing I say is getting through to either of you. I'll see my way out." He forced his black felt hat onto his head so hard it dented in the middle. As he turned and walked away, both she and Matthew looked at each other with grins pulling at their mouths. When the front door banged shut, they both burst out in laughter. "Shh..." Ruby whispered to her son. "We don't want him to hear us. We're in enough trouble as it is."

Carly decided to keep her presence a secret, but darn she wanted to cheer Matthew on, but more Ruby for being smart enough to put everything in her son's name. And here, I thought the Amish led simple, idyllic lives. They worked hard and put up with a system of control that was very one-sided.

She had a feeling that Bishop Yoder was going to try and take the farm away from them. Matthew's ownership appeared to stop him flat. Carly felt so relieved Matthew was independent and stood up to the man.

We really need to find Hannah, they will be perfect together if her father is any indication of the girl's self-worth. Besides, after the way Matthew handled the Bishop today, she didn't think he would want a woman that didn't stand up to the obstacles they faced.

With that thought Carly rose from the step, she needed to get ready for Ash and the others to arrive. Matthew asked Ash to meet them here so he could show them the paths that Hannah used on a regular basis. David agreed it would be a good starting point.

She decided to leave mother and son alone and come down once Ash pulled up. Carly worried about the bishop stopping them from investigating the area and buildings. David said he and Ruben would contact their neighbors, Carly hoped they didn't need the support, but they probably would. "There is something wrong with that bishop. Maybe he has dementia. Children always come first."

Moon Pies

Ingredients
For the cookies
1/2 cup unsalted butter softened
1/2 cup granulated sugar
1/4 cup packed light brown sugar
1/2 teaspoon salt
1 large egg
1 egg yolk
1 teaspoon vanilla
1 and 3/4 cups flour
1 tablespoon cornstarch
For the filling
2 tablespoons water
2 tablespoons light corn syrup
1/3 cup granulated sugar
1 egg white room temperature
1/2 tablespoon gelatin powder
1 tablespoon cold water
1/4 teaspoon vanilla
For the chocolate glaze
12 ounces semisweet chocolate chopped
1 tablespoon vegetable oil
Instructions
Make the cookies

In a large mixing bowl, beat the butter, sugars, and salt together with an electric mixer on medium speed until well combined. Add the egg, egg yolk, and vanilla; beat until incorporated.

In a medium bowl, whisk the flour and cornstarch together. Add it to the butter mixture and beat until fully incorporated. Gather the dough into a ball, cover with plastic wrap and refrigerate for at least 2 hours.

Preheat the oven to 350°F. Scoop 1 tablespoon sized pieces of dough and roll them into balls. Place the balls of dough 2 inches apart on a baking sheet lined with parchment paper. Bake for 10 to 12 minutes or until the edges of the cookies are lightly browned.

Cool on the pan for 5 minutes, then transfer to a wire rack to cool completely.

Make the filling

Combine the water, corn syrup, and sugar in a small saucepan fitted with a candy thermometer. Bring to a boil and cook to "soft-ball" stage, about 235°F.

Meanwhile, in a large bowl, beat the egg white on medium speed until soft peaks form.

Sprinkle the gelatin over the water and set aside to soften. Once the syrup reaches 235°F, add in the softened gelatin and mix until fully dissolved. With the mixer running on low, slowly pour the syrup into the beaten egg white. Add the vanilla. Turn the mixer to medium-high speed and continue to beat until stiff. (This may take around 3-5 minutes)

Transfer the marshmallow to a pastry bag fitted with a round tip. Pipe a large kiss of marshmallow on the bottom side of half the cookies. Top with a second cookie to form a sandwich. Refrigerate for 30 minutes.

Make the glaze

Add chocolate and oil to a heatproof bowl and set it over a pot of barely simmering water. Stir constantly until chocolate is melted and smooth.

Working with one cookie at a time, use a fork to dip it into the bowl of melted chocolate. Flip it over to fully coat the cookie in chocolate.

Tap off any excess and let it drip back into the bowl. Place the cookies on a wire rack set over a large baking sheet. Refrigerate until chocolate is set.

Keep cookies stored in the refrigerator until ready to serve. Cookies with keep for up to 3 days stored in an airtight container.

Chapter 7

The arrival of the police seemed to rocket through the community. Many of the searchers were outside with Ash's force. Carly heard Ash tell the fathers that Matthew would be leading the men to the paths the girls would have followed that night. She felt relief that it hadn't rained since last night, so they would be able to scan the area for evidence.

Carly didn't realize that the song meeting, called a "singing," was held at the Eischler's barn. Whatever happened to the two girls must have taken place there or close to it.

Matthew told the searchers earlier that Hannah and Mary were at the singing, but when he went to get Hannah, she was nowhere to be found. He didn't realize at the time that Mary was missing as well. He thought Hannah must have walked home. All the farms in their district were close, within one or two miles from each other. Walking was easy as pathways were leading through the fields.

It was odd that Ruby's farm was so near the Fisher's property. The Fisher home appeared nothing more than another house on Ruby's property.

Carly and Ruby refilled the coffee cups as the men sat around the table hashing out their plans.

Carly looked over at Ruby and tried to smile to ease the lady's nervous state. First the Bishop, and now the police descended on her home. The men finished their meeting and left the kitchen to start the search.

"Ruby, should we follow them?" Carly really wasn't sure of the right way with the Amish. So far, she's been dealing with a whole new outlook of them. She didn't realize they were as secretive and close-knit as they were. She couldn't find her bearings as to what to say and do. She let Ruby take the lead, and she followed the woman.

Ruby shook her head. "*Nee,* we should stay here. Matthew will let us know if there is anything to be found."

Carly bit her tongue. She wasn't used to this submissive female role. Waiting had never been her strong suit.

Ruby dropped down on a wood chair. "It sounds as if they are going to backtrack on the path leading to the Eischler's, but the searchers already did that. Carly, what can they find that the searchers didn't?"

"I doubt if they find much of anything. As Matthew told them the path is used by many people besides just Hannah."

"Will the searchers have destroyed anything useful?"

"Unfortunately, they probably did."

"Why don't we go to the sitting room and wait to hear any news Matthew and the detective bring back?"

The women walked through the kitchen then made a right turn into the vast room. Carly used the stairs right off the kitchen that lead to the upper floor where her bedroom was located, but she'd not explored this "sitting" room. It would hold one hundred people and then some. She turned to Ruby and asked,

"Why is this so large? What do you use it for?"

"One of the main things is church services. We have services every other week. Our turn comes about once a year or so. Each Amish home has a large sitting room. If they don't, their barn is cleaned top to bottom, and the services are held there."

Carly closed her mouth on the explanation. She watched Ruby pick up some yarn and decided she may as well run upstairs and get her own.

"I'll be right back, I need to get my project."

When Carly came back down, she found Ruby sitting in a cozy alcove tucked away off the side of the sitting room. It was big enough for two chairs with a footstool each.

"Come, sit down," Ruby said to Carly. "What is it you're working on? I didn't expect that a busy *Englisch* woman would have an interest in crochet."

"My grandmother taught me to crochet when I was around five. I've been doing it ever since as it helps me to relax. This is a blanket for someone that needs it, I give them to the church to distribute."

"OH! You are a church woman?"

"Does it surprise you that many *Englisch* are part of one religion or another." Carly smiled at Ruby's rather confused look. "I take it the Amish think we are heathens."

Ruby peered down at her crochet, her hand speeding faster at her work showing her nervousness. "It is terrible for me to think that *Englisch* are not strong in their faith or to have no faith at all. We, and I mean Amish in general, think poorly of your kind. I should ask forgiveness in my prayers tonight. It's not usual for me to meet many like you, Carly."

"I, too, have some preconceived ideas about the Amish." Carly took a breath and looked at Ruby, "but they are quickly changing."

The women smiled at each other. Ruby offered her crochet up for Carly to see. "I'm making a sweater for my sister for Christmas. She's the first one on my list so I'm starting the year early so I can have them done. I knit as well. I'll make a knit sweater for Matthew. Anything else I make in between, I put in the store to sell there."

"I see you are using the afghan stitch like mine. People don't realize how versatile crocheting actually can be."

"We've been at this a long time," Ruby said. The dull sound of footsteps came from the mudroom and then the back door slammed as someone else went through the door. Matthew must have come in first. People not accustomed to that door didn't know it shut with a bang.

In a few moments, Matthew and the detective came into the sitting room looking for them.

"Over here," Ruby called, "we are doing needlework by the window."

Ruby stood. "Do you two need some *kaffe*? The pot is still nearly full from earlier. I can reheat some for you."

Carly moved a little slower than Ruby to put up her blanket. She couldn't seem to take her eyes off Ash. His dark, coffee colored hair was tousled from the wind, and his well-defined cheekbones held a red tint to them. Being outside worked well for him, she didn't remember how appealing he could look to her. Their breakup did not go well, but it happened.

Her study of him earned a smile across his rugged features. She didn't realize he stayed behind with her and the smirk on his full lips said he caught her perusal.

"Did you find anything interesting?" His deep voice vibrated through her like it used to do months ago.

"Actually, yes, it must be getting cold out, your face looks windblown."

"It might rain again."

He held out his hand to help her up. Carly hesitated then placed her petite hand in his large palm. She let him help her stand up, and together they headed for the kitchen. Ruben Eischler came in the back door as they walked into the kitchen.

Carly's lip was sore from all the biting to keep her questions silent. Ruby and herself weren't even sitting at the table with the men, in fact, she figured the men could care less if they stayed standing in the mudroom or not. *I am going to give Ash a sharp talking to when this meeting is over.*

Oh, she wanted to scream at them all. Nothing was found, not one little piece of evidence. Carly caught the change in the discussion and moved closer to the kitchen sink. Ruby tried to stop her, but Carly brushed her hold away. She felt Ruby move up beside her as the talk around the table became heated.

"The man should have joined us, at least invite us inside as the rain started." Carly could see the veins on David's forehead throbbing under his tempered words. It seemed the Bishop overstepped himself.

Mary's father stood to speak. "*Siss ken fa-sjtant!*"

Ruby turned around to look at the *mann*. "What makes no sense Mr. Eischler?"

"Bishop Yoder! He didn't help on the search. He said the girls ran off to the *Englisch*."

David ran his hands through his blond hair that was damp with the recent rain and from sweat. His face was even paler than his usual creamy light tan. "*Nee! M*y daughter did not run off. None of her clothes was missing, she even had money stashed in her hope chest. It proves she did not leave on her own."

"Tell that to Bishop Yoder," Matthew interjected. "This time he is mistaken, but he will not admit to it. He always has to be right,"

Ruben Eischler shook his head. "*Nee,* Matthew, we must not speak of the Bishop this way. He is our leader, he knows the best. We must pray about this. *Be not hasty in thy spirit to be angry: for anger resteth in the bosom of fools.*"

"As one of our district's ministers, Ruben, you are too kind to the bishop in this matter." David stood and paced back and forth across the kitchen. "I will ask *Gott* to forgive me and to help us find our girls, but as far as the bishop goes, I will pray for him to ease his grip on his ego."

"Ok men," the detective interjected. "This is getting us nowhere. We will have to put out an amber alert for the girls. At this point, that's all we can do."

The men stood dejectedly and readied to return to their homes.

"Ruby, thank you for your hospitality," David spoke. "Miss Laine, thank you for all your help and guidance as well. I will keep everyone informed if I hear something or if Hannah returns home." He dipped his head and placed his straw hat on his head and turned toward the mudroom door.

The other men followed him out the door. All except Matthew who dropped into a chair.

"Oh no, you don't Mr. Folsham!" Carly rushed to the door to meet up with Ash before he left, she still needed to discuss some things with him, especially his chauvinist attitude.

Chapter 8

Ruby's head pounded. Exhaustion. Worry. Fear. The feelings all rolled up into a ball of anxiety. Would this day ever end?

First, she found out Hannah was missing, and seeing Matthew's distress was terrible enough. Then second, Hannah's best friend was missing as well. She knew Mary Eischler since she was born, but Mary was a child in Ruby's eyes. How these *kinner* grew into young adults so quickly was beyond her.

She didn't think Hannah would run away. She had no reason to do so, not with her courtship with Matthew. The girl was always smiling or humming a hymn under her breath.

Hannah's friend, Mary was to be the new teacher at their school in the fall, but would Hannah go with her friend if Mary needed her? Hannah was so sensitive and loving.

Ruby looked at the clock that was beside her large calendar, the only decoration in the kitchen. It was eight o'clock. She pulled out her cell phone from behind her apron. She would text Matthew to come over. She so needed someone to talk to.

The spinning of her mind left questions. Why hadn't she thought of all this before when the men were sitting at her table? Quickly, she tapped on the glass of her phone, no bigger than a deck of cards. Technology interested her; another secret she kept. She understood why her plain people were discouraged from using the *Englisch* ways. They made life more comfortable, and easy wasn't an Amish way as well.

Ruby sat at the table waiting for her son. Her only child. Her husband, Mark, had died six years ago. He died in town at the hardware store as he had just paid for a copper tea kettle for her. A surprise, he told the clerk, for his wife, and that they had just learned there would be a baby coming.

The woman told Ruby how happy and delighted Mark was, then suddenly, his eyes rolled back in his head, and he was gone. Just like that.

Since he died in the city, the ambulance came for him. That started the officials looking into his death. Why had a thirty-year-old dropped dead with no indication he was ill. Secretly, Ruby was thankful he had passed where he did. If he had died in their district, she never would have known what took him. Mark's parents had died right before she and Mark married in a horrible truck and buggy crash.

The autopsy showed Mark had something called an AVM in his brain, an arteriovenous malformation. A tangle of vessels he was born with. One of the arteries had burst much like an aneurysm. His death was instantaneous. It was a terrible blow to Ruby. There had been no way to know Mark had this deformity. The only hint was in his frequent headaches. He always cheered her up by pointing out everyone had headaches. Just look at the store shelves at all the different kinds of pain relievers sold there. He had joked her concerns away.

The *Englisch* medical people assured her that her *kinner* wouldn't inherit this AVM as it was a deformity and happened rarely. She trusted what they said, but she still had a fear in the bottom of her soul. It wasn't the Amish way to have tests, so she lived with the fear and her faith in *Gott*.

Sadly, days later she had lost their newly forming baby. Ruby was numb to both Mark's death and the miscarriage. All her life she wanted a large family, but with her husband's death, she cherished Matthew.

Suddenly, Matthew sat across from her. He had poured each of them meadow tea and even added ice. She had been so deep in her thoughts, she had not heard him enter the kitchen.

"Thank you, son."

Matthew smiled at her. "What did you need to talk to me about?"

He looked tired. His eyes were red-rimmed and small lines radiated from their corners. He had a faint line from his nose to his mouth. At eighteen, this wasn't usual.

Ruby reached out and placed her hand on top of his. "I was thinking about Mary Eischler. Do you think Mary might have run away, and Hannah went with her to watch out for her?"

Slowly shaking his head, Matthew said, "*nee,* Mary was as happy as Hannah with her new job at the school coming in a few months. She had plans with Thomas Glick, the teacher, today actually, to meet him to take his grade books and other things now that school was out for the summer."

Taking a sip of the cold tea, Ruby formed another question. "Did anyone check where Mr. Glick was today? I don't remember seeing him in the search party when I was over at the Fisher's earlier."

Matthew took a sip of his iced tea and leaned back into the chair and stretched his legs out. "No. He wasn't there. I wondered about it at the time, but I had not thought of it again until you mentioned it." He drank his tea, then stood. He walked to a cabinet beside the back door where she kept her notepads, recipes, and other such office items. "Shall we keep a list of our questions to ask the authorities the next time they are here?"

Ruby nodded in agreement. "I think it would be better if one of us took the list to David Fisher as well. Probably, he will have many if not more questions than we do."

Matthew yawned. "I think I should head toward home. My eyes don't want to stay open."

"I have the same feeling. Son. I'm so sorry this is happening to you. I share with you the Bible verse running through my mind. *Trust in him at all times, you people; pour out your hearts to him, for God is our refuge.*"

Matthew nodded and closed his eyes. His distress broke Ruby's heart. To break the sadness she said, "I have not heard our guest return, so I'll leave on a light near the stairway for her."

Matthew stood and hugged her goodnight, and both went their own directions to turn in for the night. Walking to her suite on the other side of the sitting room made her feel as if she were walking through a vat of pudding. So sluggish. She was thirty-six and felt eighty-three tonight.

Chapter 9

"Wait up, Ash." Carly never could keep up with him. His long stride seemed to increase when he was going over information on a case. She wanted to know what he really thought about the missing girls. Ash is the type of guy that keeps everything inside. At one point they shared everything. Unfortunately, that same trust ruined their partnership and personal relationship.

Deep in her own thoughts, Carly suddenly hit the solid wall of Asher's chest. "I thought you got over running into me."

Carly could feel her cheeks flare in embarrassed heat. The hold he maintained on her upper arms kept her from stepping back and away. But nothing stopped her from seeing the humor lighting his deep blue eyes.

They stared at each other for a while until he finally let go of her.

"What did you want, Carly?"

"What...I-I want you to talk to me. Tell me what you think. Did you learn anything?"

"The only thing I learned is that nothing has changed with them."

Carly swallowed her gasp, *of course, how could she forget?* "I am sorry. I should never have brought you into this mess."

"Yeah, well, it isn't your fault. My father was actually in the search party, and he never acknowledged my presence."

She let a few cuss words fly loose that earned his deep guff. "After all this time they should be over it. This shunning business is terrible and unjust. The bishop threatened Ruby and her son with shunning."

"What? For what reason?"

She could hear his concern and outrage, "The only reason I could gather is that they are more involved in the *Englisch* than he liked.

Personally, I think he is ticked that they are more independent than most the Amish I have seen here. I am not sure how long Ruby has been on her own raising Matthew, but she's done a fine job of it, and that bishop should be applauding her not attacking her."

Carly felt the constriction leaving her chest as Asher finally started to smile. He placed his index finger under her chin and raised her head to look at him. "I wonder how Ruby would feel knowing she has such a strong supporter on her side."

"She would probably say I am an *Englisch*."

She forgot how incredible this man's laughter could be. "The lady is full of surprises."

They both gathered their thoughts for a moment. Carly decided now wasn't the time to scold him for being so chauvinistic to her. She would put it away for another time. The thought there would be another time surprised her.

Before she could think any more on it, she asked, "What do you feel happened to the girls?"

"I don't know. Running away is not an option for these girls, they both have a future and happiness before them. People don't leave when they enjoy their lives here."

Regret? Yeah, she could hear it in his words. "If they didn't run where the heck are they?"

"That is the ultimate question, and I have no answer for it. I do think the girls are still in this area. Let's face it, if they were in a city, there are a lot of Amish that left their communities who are looking out for the runaway youth, so they would stand out."

"So, these watchers would let you know?"

"Yes, I have already put out notices for them to watch for the girls. So far no one has contacted me, and I know they would."

"What can we do?"

"Not much, just keep an eye out for anything unusual."

"Oh, could you look into the teacher, Mr. Glick? He is never around for anyone to question."

"I have him on my list, I too thought it odd that he wouldn't be looking for them, especially Mary."

"That is what threw up the flags for me, I mean he is teaching her to take over in the new term. And Ash, what about the bishop? There is something really off about that man and his reaction to all this."

"He is still as mean as I remember him, and that is nothing unusual for me."

"I guess that answers a lot of questions."

"Hey, don't stop noticing these things, your gut was always right when we worked cases together."

She smiled up at him, "Yeah, well, I think I am out of practice."

"Do you mind telling me why you're even here in this community?"

She worried her lip wondering if she should tell him, but he did ask, "I came here to help me heal from my last case." Carly looked up at him and knew she didn't mistake the troubled look he held her in.

"That wasn't your fault, and you know it."

"It was. I should never have come to you and the force for help. I should have just gone by myself to make the trade...."

Ash took hold of her shoulders and gave her a small shake, "No, we were wrong, we didn't listen even when you insisted it had to be you to go to the pickup place." He pulled her into the shelter of his chest, she couldn't keep the sobs back no matter how hard she tried.

"Come on, Carly. I doubt if that bastard ever meant to give her back. Did you know that the actual time of death was a couple hours earlier?"

Carly stepped back and stared at him. "No, I didn't know that."

"No, you probably didn't as you made it very clear that no one at the station was to contact you...for anything."

"Oh, so they did listen to my ravings, nice to know."

"Hey, let it go, sweet girl, just let it go." Ash didn't ask and just pulled her back to him. He felt so comforting and safe, yes safe, he always felt that way to her.

She didn't care if it started raining or the world suddenly turned inside out, Carly wrapped her arms around him and stayed buried in his warmth. The feel of his hand running down her back made her sigh, and question why she ever left his sheltering hold.

"Hey, let's go get some dinner, I am running on empty."

"Okay, I'll go in and let Ruby know I won't be here for dinner."

Carly and Ash sat at an Amish diner in the small town of Paradise Wells. She listened to Ash rattle off the dinner order and never once thought to stop him or contradict what he ordered for her. No, Carly decided she was under some sort of spell and almost laughed over thinking Ruby was a secret Amish witch.

When she felt him staring at her, she couldn't help but notice how cute he looked. Oh yes, Asher could still light a fire inside of her.

"What..." they both started talking at once. Asher held up his wine glass, "You first, Carly."

She refused to drop her attention from him, knowing she always read the truth in his eyes. "I wanted to know what, if anything, I should be looking for. I will be at Ruby's for a couple weeks."

His thumb caressed the top of his glass, around and back, it almost felt hypnotizing.

"Are you really staying there that long?"

She nodded and smiled over his disbelief.

"You will get bored."

"I don't think so, so far it has been awe-inspiring." Carly giggled over the look he gave her. "Besides Asher, where can I work on a case and get a small vacation at the same time?"

"I guess, but when she has you shoveling the cow patties don't say I didn't warn you."

She could feel the heat creep up her neck over the image, she'd argue the point but who knows, Ruby could do it.

"All kidding aside, keep a watchful eye out. If someone in the community took the girls, they could be very dangerous."

"I thought about that, but who would do something like this?"

"Hard to say, but that might be the only answer we have."

"We need to find them."

His large hand reached across the table to cover her tapping fingers. It felt odd to have him touching her again, but honesty made her admit it was a nice feeling.

"Hey, you need to back off it a bit. These people won't talk to you if you come at them like a hammer. Just be yourself and talk to people, believe me, if they have something to say they will."

"Ash, why did you leave the community? I mean I know you said it was because of your desire to be a detective, but there must have been more to be shunned."

He sat back in his chair, and she could tell he remembered that day. Carly waited for him to come back to her.

"It was all over a girl."

"Wow, I never expected that."

He smiled sadly at her, "I was a very handsome seventeen-year-old Amish boy."

She scrunched her nose at him, "I can believe that."

"Of course, she was Amish as well, from the next community west of Lancaster. I met her in town during our *rumspringa*. When he stopped talking, she looked up at him, "there is more, isn't there?"

"Yes."

He took a deep breath before starting again.

"She announced to her parents that she was pregnant and they, in turn, got a hold of my father."

"Oh, no."

"Oh yes, she remained adamant I was the father despite my denials."

"Why did she lie?"

"I never really found out. I've thought about it a lot, and the only thing I can think of is that she was protecting the real father."

"But no one believed you." She didn't need his answer it was written all over his face.

"No, my father refused to even listen to my side. I think that hurt the most. I already knew the outcome, the bishop was very vocal about kicking the ill denier out of their midst.

And that was it, I left that night and never looked back."

"Dang, the whole affair sounds so unfair."

"I thought that at first, but it was probably the best thing I could do. I doubt if I would have liked staying in the community. The bishop and I would probably have clashed anyway."

"Yes, I don't think you would stand to be ruled by such a rotten person."

"He is still the same angry man, maybe even worse. He has no intention of looking for the girls."

"I don't understand him, nor the people for following such a ridiculous claim that the girls left on their own. They wouldn't do it, Ash."

"No, I don't believe they would."

At that, he ordered them both to eat their dinner before it got cold.

Carly didn't bring up the community or the girls again. They both enjoyed a lighter conversation.

Chapter 10

The sun barely brightened the sky when Ruby rolled onto her side and looked out the window. It was five a.m. the time she always woke up. When she was a child, she had to help with the milking and gathering eggs each morning. She and her sister, Miriam, exchanged the chores weekly. Ruby enjoyed milking much more than the chickens. They always pecked at her hands as she searched for the eggs. She went to school with scabs and blood spots on her hands during this chore week.

Their brother, Isaac was older than both sisters. Ruby was eighteen when both her parents fell ill to a virus that spread through their area. Both died within days of each other. Isaac continued to run the farm, but it was small. The acres didn't bring in much money so when Ruby married Mark Troyer, Miriam, two years younger than Ruby, moved in this haus with Ruby and new husband. Isaac sold the family farm, married and moved to Ohio where land was plentiful.

Miriam had not found the right *mann* to marry until last year at age thirty-three, but her sister was happy in her new role as a wife.

Now, Matthew took care of the chores. He loved his chickens, cows, pigs, sheep, and goats. The farm was a menagerie of animals. An authentic farm, the animals provided them with food throughout the year. Ruby even made soap twice in the summer for their farm visitors. It brought in many customers to the farm, and the soap was sold in the store near the farm stay *haus*.

Images of the store brought back thoughts of David Fisher to her mind. She was both aggravated and sorry for the *mann*. A week had passed, and Hannah and her friend Mary were still missing.

Ruby said her silent morning prayers and asked *Gott* to keep the girls safe and help them to return home safely.

Tossing off the covers, she slid from the bed and to her bathroom next door. As the warm water from the shower covered her, rinsing the soft smelling soap and shampoo from her body, guilt filled her soul. She saw herself in the Bishop's eyes. He was right. She had become an *Englisch* person masquerading as Amish. Her home was as plain as she could make it but modern enough for guests. No, she didn't offer television and Internet connections, but electricity filled the walls of the old home with its wonders.

Ruby dried off, dressed and twisted her waist-length red hair into a figure eight bun and attached it to her head with bobby pins. Then next came her *Kapp,* pinned on as well. Surprisingly, her hair held no traces of white. Her Mammi's hair was very red when she passed at age eighty-eight. Taking a deep breath to fortify her for the day, she opened the bathroom door, walked down the hallway to the steps making her way to the kitchen.

Orange and yellows from the sunrise streamed into the kitchen. Ruby loved late spring mornings like these. May was her favorite month of the year. She made *kaffe*, then started making bread. By six a.m. she had six loaves rising.

While kneading the bread, she came up with the idea to help David Fisher and his young daughter and son. Twins. Hannah was the oldest child, and she was the primary person in the household that cooked. Ruby finished up her cup of *kaffe*, squeezed a bag of oranges into a plastic pitcher, and snapped on the lid. Then she went to the mudroom and grabbed her black cape from a hook. She walked out the door and headed to the neighbors. She'd cook breakfast for the Fisher's.

David Fisher rounded the corner of his barn as Ruby knocked at his back door. "Ruby Troyer, can I help you with something?"

She held up the pitcher of orange juice. "Fresh squeezed. I brought it, and myself. I will cook for you and your *kinner* a nice breakfast."

"I have eggs." David held up the basket showing Ruby his offering.

They laughed together as David opened the door and led her into the kitchen.

"I like the changes in here, David. It's so different than when my grandparents lived here, and my brother after them." Ruby opened the new refrigerator and placed the orange juice on the top shelf.

David opened the oven door, then donned mitt potholders. "I made baked oatmeal for breakfast. We'll have eggs and your *wunderbarr* juice to go with it. I'll go wake Daniel and Sarah. With their sister missing they have been through so much. I let them sleep in today."

"You go. I'll start us more breakfast. I saw bacon when I opened the refrigerator. Would you like that with the eggs and oatmeal? Ruby found she was talking to the walls. David had gone for his young ones.

When the three Fisher's came into the kitchen, Sarah and Daniel Fisher called *gute mariye* to her. They smiled, but it didn't reach their eyes. She could see sadness all over them.

"Let's pray so we can partake of Ruby's good food." David bowed his head in silent prayer.

He talked to his *kinner* as if they were adults, telling them there was no news of their sister. They looked down at their plates but didn't reply. "I also did your chores this morning. You may have this morning to do as you like. Finish breakfast and go play."

"Really, *Daed*?" Daniel asked. He bounced in his chair. "I am making a tetherball pole behind the barn, so we and our friends can play. Is it ok if I use some of your dry cement mix when I have the pole done? Matthew will come over and bring his small welder to attach a loop for us when he has time."

"Calm down son. I didn't know about this game you are fixing up. Where are you getting a tetherball in the first place?"

Daniel looked his father in the eye, then nodded at Ruby. "Her son Matthew gave us a piece of steel and a tetherball he had come across at the Rigler's auction about a month ago. He said he'd help us get it all rigged up. It is ok, isn't it, *Daed?*"

"*Jah,* it's fine. If you need help just ask me."

"I will," Daniel said. "Can I be excused?"

His father nodded.

Sarah chimed in, "Me, too?"

He nodded again.

Both *kinner* ran from the *haus*, the screen door banging behind them.

"Do not follow them, Ruby," A smile pulled the corners of his mouth into a silly grin.

She laughed, then stacked the dishes into a pile. "Since you did the *kinner's* chores, I won't leave you with anymore. You go do what you need to get done, and I'll *ridd* up the kitchen."

"Sit. The only thing I need to do is talk to you."

Ruby's felt her stomach drop. She feared he wanted to bring up moving or knocking down the store again. "I don't know what to do about the store. Please. Why can't you drop this?"

David sat with his elbows on the table and dropped his head into his hands. "That topic is not why I want you to stay. I like your company. Truly, I am sorry about the store building," he mumbled. He looked up at her and Ruby saw the fatigue lining the corners of his eyes, and the droop of his skin. "I need the entrance off the highway. The highway department will only grant a certain number of access roads from the highway. They are all used, and I can't get one. I need the access where the store sits. It's the only way to reach the new barn I'm going to put up."

So that was the problem. Ruby's eyes burned with unshed tears. She felt so guilty. "I don't know what to say. I have been so angry with you about the store."

"And I with you as well, Ruby. I see no solution to our problem."

Ruby took a sip of her cold *kaffe*. "If you give me a few days, I may have a solution to this dilemma."

"Really? How?"

Ruby shook her head. "I'll let you know if it works out, but I don't want to get your hopes up."

David nodded. "I'm to be on my knees tonight asking for forgiveness of my anger toward you. Can you forgive me, Ruby?"

She smiled at him and nodded. "Of course. Can you forgive me as well?"

"*Jah,* we are neighbors. We have to get along, and that brings up another matter."

"Is this about my *Englisch* customer?"

"Ruby quit guessing. You are getting this all wrong. It does have to do with the police involvement in Hannah and Mary's disappearance, but not with your customer. It has to do with the detective. I've heard he is Amish."

Ruby nodded. "Shunned a few years back."

"That doesn't matter, once Amish, always Amish."

"It is a sad thing. I know Asher's parents. His mother has been destroyed by it all. She was once involved in quilting's and our canning groups. Now she keeps to herself at her home and seldom talks to anyone after church. Her husband is one of the ministers in our district. Bishop Yoder was instrumental in Asher's shunning."

"How old did you say he was when this happened?"

"I believe he was seventeen."

"Not baptized then. Asher could come back if he asked the Bishop and community with a kneeling confession."

Ruby stood, "Would you like some more *kaffe*?"

David nodded and continued. "So, tell me, what was his crime against Gott?"

Pouring the *kaffe* into first David's cup then hers, she walked back to the stove and sat the percolator on the burner then turned the knob on the front to off.

"He fell in love with the wrong girl."

David uttered a laugh under his breath. "Sorry, I know it's not funny, but how many of our boys have been lured away by love?"

Ruby sat, then moved her fingers over the rim of her mug as she thought about his question. "It was a terrible situation. The girl and her family had moved here a few months before, and suddenly, Asher was courting her. Then, the rumors began to fly about her being with child. That was the reason Asher took off with her. *Ach*! His mother tried to reason with him before he left, but he wouldn't listen. His father on the other hand was a stern man and didn't even try to listen to the boy.

Asher even swore to his family that he wasn't the father, but he was so in love, he felt he had to protect this girl Selena Dickenson.

After he left and was shunned, his parents found out he had passed his GED and had applications to college to study criminal justice. He must have done that because look at him now. A lead detective."

"Your tale is a sad one, Ruby. What happened to the girl?"

Ruby shook her head. "I heard tell that she lost the baby and then left Asher."

"But he didn't return home?"

"*Nee,* he didn't. I suppose he loved his job and the *Englisch* ways."

Chapter 11

Carly came to wonder how she found this window in her room to be such a calming catalyst in her current situation. "Still nothing on them. Where are they?" she took a deep breath to reclaim the quiet place once again. She couldn't shake the feeling they missed some vital piece of this ongoing puzzle.

Ash's call this morning only confirmed the lack of information about the girls. He exhausted all his contacts for any info and neither girl had been seen anywhere around this area. Carly instinctively knew that was a horrible sign. If something didn't show up soon, they were going to lose these two young girls.

She spotted Ruby coming back from David's and waved to her. Her friend certainly stayed a long time at the man's place. The thought brought a rare glimmer of pleasure to Carly. "Might be a romance in the air."

Funny how that thought brought Ash to mind. He wanted to rekindle their relationship, Carly knew him well, and yes, she did miss him in her life. "But...I can't."

Carly could hear Ruby moving around downstairs, and she wanted the company. One thing she found she liked to do with Ruby was cook. The lady already taught her so many new dishes and how she could pare them down for just her or a smaller number to feed.

"I do like how they all come together and share everything, good or bad."

Carly moved away from the window and gathered her sweater to go join Ruby. She'd been here a week already, and it indeed wasn't what she expected.

"Carly, hello! On the way back from David Fisher's *haus* I was thinking about you. Then I saw you wave from the window."

Once in the kitchen, Ruby began pulling out ham, mustard, and bread to make sandwiches. Once she had them wrapped in waxed paper she reached up to the space between the top of her cabinets and the ceiling, taking down a picnic basket.

She placed two frozen water bottles in a basket, put ham sandwiches on top and two apples. "We have done so little since you arrived. I usually take my guests on planned farm experiences. Would you like to go on a walk and see the farm?"

"I would love to see the farm. Let me run up and get my other shoes on."

"I'll gather a few more things to add to the basket while you do that."

The sky looked so blue out here in the open hills. Carly breathed in the fresh air as she followed Ruby down the dirt path. The fields were bright spring green with all the new crops coming up. She'd been surprised over how many types of vegetables they planted.

"Our land goes clear across the hill to the trees on the east border. We have many more acres to the north, and of course, you know that David Fisher's place starts where the store is located."

"I remember the for-sale sign. Have you two figured out how to settle the problem?"

"*Jah,* we have discussed the problem he has. You see, he needs the space for an entrance to his property. There are not enough access points, and the state won't issue anymore. I plan on our walk to check near the trees for access on the road near them. I remember we used to come into the property from the backside during the winter when the snowstorms kept us from using the main highway."

"I hope we can find it. I can always go into town. The courthouse keeps maps of every piece of property and any easements on the land. I can make copies of the maps for you and David."

"That would be wonderful. Our hunt today will show us a lot, and I can tell David Fisher to ease his concerns." She looked down at the dirt path and continued, "And mine as well." Switching her basket to her other arm, she looked over at Carly. "Have you been to the store since you've been here?"

"No, I haven't really had time to go anywhere."

"And you came here to rest." Ruby laughed lightly. "I will show you the farm today, and you can rest tomorrow. I'll let you be."

"I can come down to the store tomorrow. Do you have quilts? I need one for next winter."

"*Jah,* we do, but they are costly. Many shoppers complain about the prices. There are many hours to create the quilt on top of the fabrics and notions."

"I don't mind the price because I know they are hand done, that is what counts on my end."

"You are a kind woman, Carly Laine."

Carly stopped with Ruby as they topped the rise and just took in the beauty of it all. "My goodness, you are so fortunate to have all this, it is breathtaking."

Carly scanned the fields. "We should have lunch then find that road." She came to a stop, something caught her attention. "Ruby? Do you see that patch of blue?" Carly pointed to the area.

"Down this hill and over to the right? About midway to the trees?" she asked. "The ground drops so it's not easy to see."

"Yes, I think I see something."

"Do you want to explore or eat? I'd like to see what's over there. Maybe someone else had a picnic and left their blanket in the cornfield."

"I say we need to check it out before we eat."

Ruby nodded and started down the hill. Carly fell in step with her, glad she changed into her walking shoes as they didn't slip over the loosely graveled country road.

Panting a bit, Ruby pulled up then stopped. "Hang on, I need to rest a moment. I think I packed too much in the basket or else I'm getting old."

"You are not old, Ruby." Carly's soft laughter floated on the breeze.

"I will go on while you rest." Carly took the basket from Ruby and sat it on the ground then started down the hill, she needed to move over the corn rows to head in the direction of the blue patch. She walked carefully between the rows not to crush the small shoots. As she drew nearer to the blue spot, she felt a sick lump start in her stomach. "Don't let it be one of the girls," she whispered.

Carly groaned as the item took shape, it was a body that looked like a man. "Looks too big for one of the girls." She stepped over the last row of corn. Her steps were slow as she studied the ground near the body, not wanting to ruin any evidence. Carly stopped about ten feet from the bloated remains. "Yes, it is a man."

"*Ach*!" Ruby cried. "It's the teacher, Thomas Glick."

Carly jumped, not knowing Ruby was behind her. She pulled her phone from her pocket and hit Ash's number. "We best stay back so they can investigate the area."

The phone rang, and thankfully Ash answered. "Detective Folsham."

"Ash, it's Carly. I am afraid you need to come back out here and bring the crime guys, we just found the body of the teacher, Mr. Glick. I'll give Ruby the phone to explain how to get here."

"Okay Carly, take a deep breath girl."

"Did that and it isn't helping much. Here is Ruby."

After Ruby gave him directions, she handed back the phone to Carly. "I need to get the Bishop. He must be here, or he will be angry with me. Even more so since we called the police. His place isn't very far from here, just on the other side of the trees."

"Tell him I called them after all that is what the *Englisch* would do."

Ruby took off at a run headed for Bishop Yoder.

Carly caught her breath and called Matthew. Once he answered, she explained what was happening and asked him to come for his mother's sake. She couldn't help not liking the Bishop's presence and didn't want him picking on Ruby again. "And Matthew, you best bring David with you."

Once he hung up, she slipped the phone into her pocket. She could hear the Bishop yelling at Ruby as they rode up in the open carriage. "I guess he doesn't like the police being involved, oh well, too late now."

David rushed from the barn when he heard horse hoofs and a wagon heading up his gravel driveway. His stomach fell, and he worried he'd lose the wonderful good breakfast Ruby had prepared earlier this morning.

Hannah. Had she been found? He held his breath seeing Matthew Troyer stop in front of him.

"*Maem* and Carly found a body."

"*Nee*," David whispered. He reached out for the harness on the horse to hold himself upright.

"Oh, *nee*, David. Not one of the girls. A *mann*. Thomas Glick is dead."

David shook his head, thrilled at the news, then was immediately sorry he felt this way. It was not the Amish way to think about death. Poor Mr. Glick.

"Come, he is over in our cornfield on the eastern side."

David moved his wobbling legs and walked around to the other side of the buggy and stepped in. Could there be any more bad news for this community, he wondered?

"*Grossie* mistake, *baremlich*...terrible. *Der Siffer hot zu viel geleppert.* The drunkard had just sipped too much. Fell on his head."

"How do you know about his head being injured?" Ruby snapped her head in the old Bishop's direction. His white whiskers were to his waist. She noticed they were thinning. She tried to keep her gaze from the cranky *mann*. He always spouted Bible verses but had nothing to say from *Gott* today.

"How else does a drunkard fall?" He snorted then began pounding her spirit with his strong words once again. "The authorities! Why did you call them, Ruby?"

"I didn't call them, *nee,* Carly did. She pulled out her cell phone and in seconds had her detective friend on talking with her."

"And now sirens break our quiet and disturb the animals and humans alike. We take care of our own. Or have you forgotten in your *Englisch* ways?"

Ruby didn't respond to the *mann's* accusations. They were near to where the body lay, and she jumped from the buggy in a very unladylike way. She could not handle the Bishop for one second longer.

Running up to Carly, Ruby took her arm. "I hear sirens in the distance."

Carly nodded. "I've called both Matthew and David. They should be here shortly. Matthew will stay with you or walk you home."

"*Nee!* I'm not leaving. I want to know what happened. This makes me even more concerned for our girls. Could whoever killed the teacher have done away with our *maedels*?"

"*Maedel's*?"

"*Ach,* sorry. That means girls."

"*Maem,*" Matthew called as he rushed up to her side. "Come, let me take you home. You should not be here, seeing something like this."

She shook her head and replied, "I'm a grown woman. I was here when Carly found him. I will stay here until the police take him away."

David Fisher joined the group. He smiled at Ruby, but she could see the grave concern in his eyes.

"Maybe he took the girls, and Mr. Glick got hurt in the scuffle. Then Hannah and Mary ran off," Matthew said.

Ruby shook her head. "*Nee*...if that happened, where are the girls now? They would have run home for help."

"Unless they were too frightened and felt they'd killed the *mann*. They could be in hiding." the bishop spat as he approached them. "The girls could have done this. If they are afraid, we may never see the likes of them again around these parts."

Ruby watched Matthew's face pull into lines of distress. It was bad enough his beloved was missing, but to label her a murderer was more than he could take.

Bishop Yoder turned away from the group and quickly went to the body. Carly raced toward him but didn't catch the elderly man who was sprier than some gave him credit until he was kneeling over the body.

"Bishop! You just contaminated the crime scene!" Carly hollered over to him.

The look of satisfaction on his face made Carly take a step back. She mentally shook herself and wondered what the heck the man was up to. Thankfully, the police cars and crime scene van pulled up.

She just shook her head and turned to go tell Asher what happened.

After voicing her frustration to him, he chucked her under her chin and smiled at her.

"You can't solve all the ills in the world, Carly."

She tried to smile but failed, "True, but it would be nice to find the girls before it is too late." Asher's habit of biting his lower lip didn't help her mood any. Had he learned this from her?

"We are all hoping that one. Let's see what we can find out from this poor guy." He reached into his pocket and pulled out a search warrant that made her brow raise. "The warrant is what took me a little longer. No sense going back for one. Keep the parents informed of what is happening, please. I am going to be very busy from this point forward."

"Okay. Watch your back, Asher."

He looked back at her, "I don't have to, I have you."

She did smile at his reminder over what he always said when they worked together.

Asher wanted to reach out and grab her smile to keep as a memory. Her cap of blonde curls moved gently with the breeze. The sun was bringing out her freckles, the fresh air agreed with her and brought out the beauty that she always ignored. Carly was everything to him, and it was his fault that she left him. His fault that the captain interfered with her case. He was glad that he told her about the girl's time of death, nothing would have changed it, but they didn't know that at the time.

For now, Asher would let her heal, but having her so close to the bishop raised his hackles. That man and his actions had nothing to do with *Gott* and never did. He always acted for his own reason and to hurt others. *He best stay clear of Carly.*

Carly turned and headed back up the hill to face the parents of the girls now standing with Ruby and Matthew.

They didn't have to ask, their pain was written all over their distressed faces. Carly nodded at them and then told them what the crime lab would be doing. She would keep an eye on Detective Folsham.

Carly's hands were in a tight fist as Asher approached the Bishop. She concentrated to hear what he said to the man.

"Bishop Yoder, I need to see this man's place and also the school and meeting house."

"No, you have no rights here. In fact, I should not be speaking to you. You are shunned. You do not exist."

Carly caught the tightening of Asher's broad shoulders and wondered how he kept his cool with this man.

"You are wrong as usual, Bishop." He reached in his jacket and pulled out the warrant. "This is a warrant to search all the premises that I feel are relevant to this murder and the case of the missing girls." Asher grabbed the man's hand and jammed the warrant in it.

She needed to control herself not to cheer for Asher. Though she did catch a slight smile on Ruby's lips.

Asher turned away and called Matthew and the girls' fathers over to him. He explained what he just did and why...

"The Bishop is stubborn when it comes to his responsibility. We don't like to intrude but sometimes it is necessary. Matthew can you take me to the teacher's residence, please."

David spoke up, "I would like to come with you."

"Of course, you can, and Mister Eischler as well, just let me do a search before any of you enter."

They all nodded their agreement and the men marched off. Carly looked over at the Bishop and immediately saw his anger at being denied. It bothered her that the man seemed more intent on his authority than on what was happening here.

Carly said a silent prayer to keep the girls safe until they reached them.

Ruby came up beside her.

"Well, Ruby, there is no reason to stay here. They could work into the night. Shall we go back to the house?"

"This is a true mess, *jah?*" Ruby reached down and took the picnic basket. "At least I found out about the road access. Bishop Yoder came across the road and onto the property from the entrance. When things settle down, I will tell David the good news about that."

"At least it will be good news for a change." Carly bit her lip unable to keep her worry from Ruby.

They walked along toward the barn Ruby turned to look back toward the gathering of law enforcement, but she couldn't see a thing because of the hill. "What happens next, Carly?"

"Once they are done with the investigation, they will take the evidence back to the lab to process. If they find anything, they will come back to make sure they didn't miss anything or to collect more evidence." Carly coughed a bit from all the dust from the vehicles. "Ruby, can we go to the singing next time, if it is at the same place?"

"*Nee.* Each time it is at a different home. We have a list of families who hold the services, but we can visit the barn where the last singing was held. Do you expect to find anything? Or would you like to attend the singing this Sunday? It's at the Neiswanger's a few miles from here."

"A different place won't help. I want to see where the girls were before they disappeared."

"We can do this, the last singing was at the Eischler's barn."

Carly smiled at her companion, "Good. Can we do this tomorrow?"

"We can, but I wonder if the bishop will let us snoop around. He doesn't seem to be overly fond of either of us."

"Well, let's not ask him." She laughed over the look of shock that quickly turned into a conspiratorial grin from Ruby.

Chapter 12

Asher stood by the door while the forensic unit finished up taking samples and prints around the room. Mr. Glick was a neat person, the man's organization made it easy to find some clues that might help solve his murder.

He fingered the letters in the evidence bag anxious to read them. Asher hoped it would give them a look into why someone would kill the teacher. The oddest fact plagued Asher for answers, why were all the letters from the bishop's dead wife?

Hannah's father shifted his position stopping the questions forming in his head. "They will be done shortly, David."

"*Nee*, it is not that. I can't stop worrying about Hannah. It is almost two weeks, and we have nothing...it would almost be better if she did run away."

"I doubt she would."

Matthew agreed with Asher. "*Nee*, she did not, I know this in my heart." He watched as the *mann* reached over and gripped David's shoulder to reassure him. Asher wished he could tell them something, anything, to make it better. Sadly, nothing even close to relevant has turned up during their search of the grounds and the Eischler's barn where the sing took place the night the girls disappeared. The poor man is at his wit's end trying to keep it together, though his wife regretfully, hasn't done as well.

"Why don't you two take off. I am going to be here until they are through." Asher barely managed to ignore Matthew's guffaw, one thing for sure the man he was becoming would be his own thinker. The thought made Asher smile.

David nodded, "you are right, there is nothing to accomplish here, and my *kinner* will need dinner."

"I will let you know anything I discover."

"*Jah* it will be good to know."

Matthew turned to follow the *mann*, but Asher stopped him. "Matthew, please tell Carly for me that I will stop by before heading back to the office."

"Sure enough."

Asher caught the slight smile Matthew gave him before turning to go. He wondered if he was that obvious over his feelings for Carly?

"I don't have time for this, darn it." No, he needed beyond hope to turn up something to help find the girls, every second counted against them right now. "What are we missing here?"

Carly gazed up at the bright stars in the clear night. She gave up pacing to just sitting on the porch steps waiting for Asher. A smile crossed her lips as she whispered, "he is back in my life again. It feels good."

She refused to let the past enter her thoughts. She came here to move on with life. After all her denials, Carly held the firm conviction that Asher would be part of that life.

His car pulled into the drive. Carly didn't move, waiting for him to join her. Ruby and Matthew went to bed hours ago, and their rooms were on the other side of the house.

Asher looked good walking uphill to join her. He held this stature about him that pulled on her senses. She remembered the feel of his arms about her the other day and how safe she felt. Carly admitted to herself that she missed having him close.

"I am sorry you had to wait so long."

"It's alright, Asher. It is a beautiful night. The stars are brilliant out here."

He looked up and smiled, "No city light, it makes a difference."

She hated to ask him how it went tonight. Carly waited for him to bring it up, enjoying the silence between them.

"You know, being out here will spoil you."

"Do you miss it, Asher?"

"Yes, it will always be part of my life, being here brings it all back. At least, I managed to see my mom."

"I was hoping you would find a way."

"Father was at the Bishop's tonight."

She heard his heavy sigh and wished things could be different for him. This world is unusual, even she would admit how hard it would be to go home at the end of the week.

"You didn't find anything at the Eischler's, did you, Asher?"

"Nothing that will help. But at Thomas Glick's I discovered some letters that he stored behind the stove. They were from the Bishop's wife."

"That is surprising."

"*Jah*, I need to read them to figure out their connection. Funny, no one mentioned it."

"The way things are going I doubt if they knew. No one even missed the man's presence, which I just don't understand." Carly felt her annoyance rise over the truth of it.

"It is rather odd, but then the school is out, for now, maybe they thought he went home."

"More than likely, the job was only temporary. It didn't feel like anyone really knew Glick."

"That is true, for some reason he remained a stranger to everyone. Mother said he didn't even accept supper invites from some of the parents."

"Even I find that strange."

"Maybe the letters will shed some light on the whole situation. We still failed to find anything concerning the girls. I am getting worried about them."

"I know, Matthew was very sullen tonight at dinner. Of course, Ruby feels awful for him and Hannah's father. She went over to his house when we returned home and fixed the children dinner."

"Carly, are you going home now?"

"Not until Monday."

"I best be going, lots of paperwork to get done."

She remembered how much that could be for a murder case, let alone the girls' disappearance. Carly rose when he did and walked with him to his car. "I will call you immediately if we find anything."

"Do that. Be careful Carly, someone here is behind the murder and more than likely the girl's disappearance as well."

"I know, I hope we find them and soon, for sure and certain."

Asher's mouth opened, and he started laughing. "Ruby is rubbing off on you, be careful you might become Amish." He laughed again as he entered the car. "I will call or come by to let you know what the letters tell us."

"I would like that, I sure hope they help."

Carly waved as Ash backed out of the drive and left. She took a deep breath and headed back to the porch, she decided to sit on the steps a while longer before heading up to bed.

A shooting star went streaking across the night sky. Carly closed her eyes and made a wish that they would find the girls soon.

Chapter 13

The blush of dawn tinted the window shade a light orange and pulled David from a heavy sleep. Turning onto his back was difficult. His thirty-seven-year-old body groaned at every joint and each muscle fought against him. He gazed at the white ceiling. Finally, he had slept the sleep of the dead, and his body rebelled at awakening. Night after night for the past couple of weeks, David had not slept deeply because of his concern for his missing daughter.

What day was it?

His brain stayed as lethargic as his body. Slowly coming awake he remembered. Saturday. Tomorrow marked two weeks since Hannah disappeared from the face of the earth.

Dear Gott bring her safely home to us. This was his prayer, over and over again. No other prayers passed his lips. He tried, but the phrase remained stuck like a cork in a bottle. He trusted and put all his faith in the heavenly father. Undoubtedly, there was a reason for Hannah and Mary vanishing. *Gott* only knew. Suddenly, a Bible verse flashed through his mind. *John 13:7: Jesus replied, You do not realize now what I am doing, but later you will understand.*

Was Hannah's disappearance linked to *Gott's* plan in some way?

Thirty minutes later he was in the barn finishing the milking. The *kinner* would be up shortly, and he would have eggs, bacon, and toast ready. The last jar of strawberry preserves was in the refrigerator, the batch his wife had made before she fell ill. Why was it today he felt everything closing in on him? Breathing in the warm, late spring air filled his lungs but releasing it felt labored. Was this depression? He had heard of it but never thought he'd experience it himself. Maybe it was so many things culminating at one time. His wife's death, moving to a different district, losing Hannah.

No more feeling sorry for himself. David had to take care of the family. He entered the kitchen and placed the two milk buckets on a counter just inside the door. It was the milk station where David separated the milk and cream. Milk for daily use and the cream he would have the *kinner* churn into butter once a week. Ruby bought quarts of cream for her farm stay. She made all sorts of fantastic food for her customers. She had done well for him and the *kinner* the past days with Hannah gone.

Hannah. He wouldn't allow himself to think of her as gone, maybe on a holiday somewhere. *Nee.* She was missing. Kidnapped. Dead? Shaking his head, he pulled himself out of the mire before he dived in and made the depression worse.

Pulling out two two-gallon lemonade pitchers from under the cabinet he poured the contents of his buckets into the jars. They would sit in the refrigerator for twenty-four hours to allow the cream to rise to the top. When it was time, he would open the tap on the front and let the skimmed milk fill another pitcher. He allowed a small bit of cream to mix with the skimmed milk to give it a bit more body and taste. The cream went into quart jars he would sell.

Sarah and Daniel bounded into the kitchen.

"What's for breakfast, *Daed*?" Daniel inquired while he pulled a chair out from beneath the table.

The scraping sound caused a shudder to run up David's spine, and strike his teeth. He shuddered. "Son, please. Go easy on the floors. They need to last."

"They are made of rock squares. I suppose they will be here until my great-grandchildren have *kinner*."

Such deep thoughts for his son of twelve. "You're right. But it makes my teeth buzz with the sound. You two go gather the eggs while I get the bacon going, then we can eat."

"*Jah daa,*" Sarah said quietly. Following her brother, the *kinner* left with the banging of the screen door off the mudroom. Why did the young ones make so much noise? Had he been that way as a youth? Smiling to himself, he remembered his mother calling out to him to quit slamming the door. Guess his *kinner* were no different from him.

After finishing breakfast, David rolled his sleeves up before putting the dishes in the soapy water. A knock came at the back door.

"Anyone about?" Ruby called through the screen.

"Come on in Ruby. My hands are wet." He felt funny flutters in his stomach just knowing Ruby would be with him a short while. "Grab a cup of *kaffe* over yonder and have a seat. I'll be done with these chores in a few minutes."

He heard something slide across the table. "I brought you two more loaves of bread. I hope you can use them."

"Thank you, *jah*. You make the lightest bread in the district!"

Ruby came to his side and opened the drawer where he kept the dish towels. She pulled out one with chicks, full-grown chicken, and roosters embroidered on them. Of course, his wife had done the needlework on them when they were first married. He didn't mind at all that Ruby used the towel. The first time one of his distant cousins reached for one before he moved here, he felt possessive and awkward toward the material. But Ruby was different. He did not mind her hands on them at all.

"With all that has gone on with the death of teacher Glick, I have not had time to tell you, I think I solved our access problem, David."

He jerked his head in her direction. She kept her gaze down at the dishes while she wiped them dry. "How so? It seems impossible."

"There is another entry from the land to 367 at the back of our properties. I thought I remembered it, and actually, that is why Carly and I were out walking the other day when we came along Mr. Glick's body."

She shuddered as she spoke the words, David's heart went out to her. It must have been awful to stumble across a body.

"You're telling me there is highway access at the back of your property?" The first excitement he'd felt in days rushed through him. Maybe he could get his large crop planted this season. It wasn't too late. Would any of his neighbors help him get the corn in the ground?

"I'll have Matthew deed it over to you. Simple as that, but you can start using it any time now. I am so glad I remembered it. There was a fence gate across it. The weeds have taken over, and it didn't resemble an opening at all. If you want, after we finish the dishes we could go out, and I'll show it to you."

"Are the authorities allowing us to go into that part of the land yet?" he asked then placed the last pan in the drainer.

"*Jah,* and if we take your small buggy, it won't take any time at all to get there. I'd like you to show me what your plans are, too." Ruby's face blushed at her request. "If that is not too forward for me to ask."

A small chuckle pulled from his throat. "I'd love to show you my ideas. I'm all finished, and we can go now if you want."

Ruby glanced at the propane cook stove splattered with grease. "Hum, I'll be ready as soon as you show me your cleaner. The stove will stick that way I'm afraid."

"You are spoiling me, Ruby," David said. "You clean and I'll go ready the buggy." He wondered at the catch in his throat as he offered the words and also, the way his pulse raced when she smiled at him. Could it be his heart was mending from the loss of his first love?

"Are you ready to go?" David asked as he poked his head around the screen door. "I have Clementine ready."

"Clementine?" Ruby said with a smile and laughter reaching out in a melodious thrill. She caught David's smile. Putting the cleaning cloth over the middle divider of the sink, she turned and walked toward him. He opened the door wider and let her go first out on the walkway created from pavers. The horse and buggy were ready and waiting. It was a good thing they each were older, or the bishop would chastise them for being together unchaperoned. Everything in their district was governed by the rules the Bishop presided over with a firm hand. Sometimes, Ruby felt in his hand was a whip. Did *Gott* want his people ruled by fear, she wondered?

David came around to her side of the buggy and gave her a hand getting in the conveyance. The small buggy was roofless, Ruby tucked her hair into her *kapp* as the wind caught it.

David turned on the bench and reached behind him. With a grunt, he grasped an umbrella and brought it to the front.

"I-I always had this handy for my wife. It's still here ready to do service for anyone in need."

"Have you used it yourself?"

"*Jah,* I have. A few times even. You never know when we'll have a cloudburst, but today we have a burst of sun and heat." David snapped the reins, and the horse trotted off. "Now where do we go?"

Ruby directed him to the north side of his small barn. "If we continue to the east, we should see ruts still in the ground. The grass has grown over it, but if we look ahead, we'll see it."

As they rode along David was silent. Ruby did not know what to offer as a way of conversation. She didn't want to bring up Hannah. She was sure the girl was not far from his thoughts.

Ruby pointed toward the tree line at a distance. "Just past the trees is the highway. No one uses it much now that the interstate went in. That is why I forgot about the access to the back of the property."

"Is that Bishop Yoder's place up the hill on the other side of the road?"

She nodded. "It is, and the central location of it is *gut* for the bishop to reach everyone quickly that live in the district."

"It looks to be a large place for one old *mann*." David pondered. He swung the buggy around the cordoned off area where Thomas Glick was found. The road, more of a trail now, was more defined in this area.

"The Bishop at one time had a large family. All five of his *kinner* were sons. They all moved to their own farms in Ohio. The prices of a property are much less there. The Bishop's wife died last summer, so he's been alone for over ten months. I think he's gotten sterner since she died. Old age and no close family must be a terrible way to live."

"I agree with you, Ruby. I'm so glad to have my *kinner*. They weren't happy when we moved here though. They are settling in some."

"Oh, David! Here I am talking about prices of land. You should know the dynamics since you came from Ohio. How is it you were able to buy our family land and the neighbors as well?" After the words came out, Ruby felt her face flush in embarrassment. "Again, how forward of me. I'm so sorry, David."

He laughed at her. "No need to worry, dear. I think you are cute when you blush."

Swallowing with difficulty, she felt her face flame even redder. Her heart leaped over David calling her *dear* and saying she was cute. His comments took her back to her rumspringa at age sixteen when she rode around with Mark.

"My farm wasn't enormous, but I also farmed my wife's family farm as well. She was an only child. When her elderly parents died and left the farm to her. With the two farms together, I had to hire men to work for me. I made a good deal of money, but my heart wasn't in it after—after..."

"You need not say any more. I understand. I lost my husband six years ago." She patted David's hand as she spoke. "Will you hire help here as well?"

"I'm not sure. We'll see how this season goes."

The road led to a heavily weeded area, and he stopped the buggy. "Is this it?"

"*Jah*. You can see the weeds entangled in what used to be a gate. The Bishop plowed his horse and buggy through here when he came the day we found Thomas Glick. As I said earlier, you can have the access. I'll trade it for you allowing me to keep my store where it is. Will this work for you?"

He nodded and pulled at his shiny blond beard. There were a few white hairs mixed in, but he looked youthful. His pink, full lips pulled into a smile. "You have solved our problem, Ruby. Thank you."

She smiled at him and wondered at her strange feelings bouncing in her stomach. "Shall we start clearing out this mess?"

"Absolutely not! You do not need to do this. We can get a closer look at it though." He jumped down from the buggy and came around to her side. He took her at the waist and swung her from her perch placing her softly on the ground.

Ruby's eyes grew wide. She felt much too old to handle such youthful feelings, but she was going to enjoy each second of it.

Chapter 14

With all the windows down in the car Asher breathed in the spring air. "*Jah*, now that smells like home."

He immediately pulled himself back. It wasn't his home and hadn't been for over fifteen years. To lose that truth would bring back the loss he dealt with and did not want to go through again.

Funny he couldn't believe that Carly just jumped into his thoughts. He remembered how she giggled like a schoolgirl on the phone this morning when he called. It didn't take him any time at all to convince her to go to lunch with him today. He smiled and hoped she would be sitting on the porch stairs again. She looked mystical the last time he saw her sitting there bathed in moonlight watching the stars.

Asher scolded himself, he knew better than to think everything that happened over the last few months was behind them. Carly could be a very complicated woman. That she blamed him for the little girl's death still hurt, but then it was his fault. "I never should have informed the captain about the ransom drop." His balled-up fist hit the steering wheel in frustration. "I still can't believe he called the FBI and didn't tell me."

He knew the captain would expect him to tell Carly if he knew. Unfortunately, everything moved too quickly to stop. He could still hear Carly's scream when she saw the sadistic kidnapper had slit the little girl's throat. The thought of terror made him want to spit. That the girl was already dead didn't dull the shameful act.

Asher wished he could change it all. The parent's devastation still made him sick with guilt. Of course, they blamed Carly. Asher straightened them out on the facts, it didn't help Carly's own feeling of guilt and sorrow over what happened. "*Gott*, I am so sorry." *Therefore, I want you to know that through Jesus the forgiveness of sins is proclaimed to you.* The Bible verse played through his mind and eased the sorrow in his soul.

Straightening his shoulders, Asher pushed the thoughts back and turned the key on them to lock them away. "Things will be different this time. We will find the girls."

As he turned into the driveway, he couldn't stop his smile overseeing her sitting on the steps. The fact that she was crocheting totally surprised him. He hadn't seen her working the yarn for a very long time, "Maybe things are healing."

He didn't get out of the car, suddenly wanting her to come to him and be with him and him alone.

Carly refused to show Asher the pleasure she felt over seeing him again. She wrapped up the afghan and walked over placing it on the table by the porch chairs. The blanket was nearly finished, she knew Ruby would like it, and Carly wanted to give her new friend a gift from her heart.

"I'm coming!" She yelled to Asher as she grabbed her purse and practically skipped down the stairs.

He was waiting by the car door like a gentleman of old and this time her smile came unbidden. "Thank you, sir." She curtsied and let him take her hand while she got into the seat.

Asher surprised her when he didn't release her hand but raised it to his lips for a whisper of a kiss to the back of it.

Neither of them said anything. Carly could only stare at him walking around the front of the car and getting into the driver's seat.

She couldn't remain silent a moment longer, "And where are you taking me, Asher?"

"I thought we would go on a picnic."

"Really?"

"Yes, I know the perfect spot on my family's farm. No one will bother us, and it is beautiful."

"Sounds perfect." Carly managed to pull her gaze away from him and watch the landscape as he drove to their destination. "It is so beautiful out here."

"I know, nothing can compare to it. The glimpses of fresh green poking through the planted rows is thrilling to see."

"What crop is that it doesn't look like corn or wheat?"

"Soybean. It is new to our farms. It has proven to be a good feed grain and food source."

"I like to eat the edamame."

"So do the cows."

Asher didn't burst out laughing until she pulled her flabbergasted look away. "I am sorry, Carly. It just popped out."

"I think we are both being sucked into this area."

Asher agreed as he turned into the dirt road that would take them to the stand of trees by the river. "We are almost there."

"Aren't you worried your father will see us?"

"No, mother told me he would be uptown with the bishop today."

"Good, I don't need one of his stony glares to take home with me."

"I know just what you mean." Asher grabbed the basket out of the trunk and came around and opened her door. "Come on, I want to show you where I used to come and hide from the world."

She took his hand and smiled, "sounds interesting."

"Oh, many a future dream flowed under these trees." He walked her through the tall weeds surprised when he found his old path remained. The place made him feel like a boy again.

Asher watched her turn in a circle taking in the beauty of the place. He could tell she enjoyed the trees. "I hear water."

"It is the river."

"Ahh, that's why the air feels cooler."

"Yes, and there is even a swimming hole just off the bank where we will have our picnic."

When Asher stopped under the trees at the top of the riverbank, she gasped. "Oh, my goodness, this is so beautiful it takes my breath away."

"Mine as well." Although, he wasn't looking at the trees and river as much as one beautiful lady. He managed to root himself to the spot and started to spread the blanket and set out the food. "Come on Carly. Let's eat then I will take you on a tour."

"Promise?"

He smiled up at her standing there with her fist balled at her hips daring him to defy her. "Of course, now come here and eat something."

They both filled their plates with the variety of food packed neatly in containers from the basket. Carly wanted to ask who did all this at her first bite, but she had a feeling she knew and kept silent.

"This is so delicious. Thank you for thinking of this place and having a picnic, it is perfect."

Carly took her last bite and laid back on the blanket looking up at the trees flowing on the breeze.

Asher followed suit and smiled, "I will tell my mother how much you enjoyed it, but then you knew she did this."

Carly turned her head and looked over at Asher, "Yes, and I am so pleased that the two of you have a relationship."

"We have, it has been difficult over the years, but she was insistent, and I am glad." Asher smiled and decided to tell her what else his mother did the day of his shunning. "I have to tell you, she was insistent about the whole thing. She berated the bishop in front of everyone at the service and threw his shunning back at him saying he was the one shunned by her, and he would never be allowed in her home again."

This time she sat up and looked at him, "wow, she is marvelous. And she didn't get shunned herself?"

Asher smiled, and his eyes twinkled. "No. Mom is friends with everyone in the community. They love her. I also think the Bishop is a bit afraid of her. Maybe he's afraid of all strong people."

"Like you?"

Asher nodded.

"My father ran after her when she stomped out of the service and tried to pull her back. She turned on him and told him in a voice loud enough for all to hear that he could join the *pompous ass* and be shunned right along with him from her home. And with that, she got in the buggy and left him standing there with his mouth open."

"Oh my, Asher how did you find this out?"

"I was there, hiding. I never expected it, but over the years I am so glad I saw it. I never told my mother I knew."

"What about your father?"

"To this day he has never had the bishop to the house. When a service is held at our farm, the ministers give the service, and the bishop stays away."

"Sounds like a smart plan."

"She really would kick him out. The farm has always been in her name, it is her family's farm, and it is in the deed that her husband cannot inherit it."

"Really? I didn't know they could do that."

"Many of the farms are like that from the older families."

Carly sat in silence a while going over what she learned.

"Carly?"

She snapped out of her thoughts, "hmm?"

"Your choice, we can take a tour or go over the letters from the bishop's wife to Thomas Glick?" Asher really didn't have to ask, the answer was easy.

"I sure hope they helped in some way."

"Well, they were full of surprises."

"You have my attention."

"It appears Thomas Glick was related to the bishop's dead wife, a cousin."

"Really? That is a surprise."

"Yes, and she was not a happy woman. Her marriage in her words..." Ash pulled the letter from his pocket, "was a living nightmare." He passed the letter to Carly and gave her time to read it.

"Did you read them all, Asher?"

"Yes, but this one is the final one she sent. The others are basically the same, she asked Thomas to come and help her leave the bishop. She tried before, and she said he threatened to lock her in the basement."

"The poor woman." Carly could only shake her head in dismay. "It says here that if she disappeared or worse, the bishop would be to blame."

Asher nodded, "From the dates on the letters and the school records I don't think Thomas arrived in time, it looks like he was two weeks late."

Carly looked up at Asher almost afraid to ask, "Do you think the bishop killed her?"

"It is all speculation at this point. We will need to exhume the body."

"And Glick?"

"If he killed once he might have killed him as well."

"Didn't the bishop know about their relationship?"

"She mentioned to Glick that he didn't know, and she wanted to keep it that way. She even told Glick about the temporary teaching position in the letter before this one."

"More than likely that is why he was late coming here. It is so sad."

Carly wanted to say more, but she didn't like making accusations without proof. But a couple things really beat around in her mind, mainly that the bishop may have killed the teacher. "Too bad we don't have his letters to his cousin."

"I figure I will need another search warrant and that won't be easy to obtain."

Neither of them spoke much after that. Asher put the letter away and offered to show Carly the place he spent his teen years. Carly wished she could forget the letters and enjoy the rest of the day with Asher, but she couldn't quiet her mind.

Chapter 15

Asher brought her back to the house at dusk, and Carly's pacing didn't slow down. She wished Ruby were home. "She must be over at David's."

She marched up the stairs to her room and plopped down on the bed. With her arm over her eyes, she willed herself to breathe slowly and to relax. All her life she dealt with migraines and if she didn't calm down the one pushing for release would win. "Come on girl this is no way to end my stay here."

When she thought about it, she felt better since she arrived. Carly hoped that once she went home, all those dark memories would stay buried. "I need to get on with my life."

The minute she said that the image of Asher came to her. He actually relaxed at the river. Carly wished she could have seen him as a kid without all the worry he now carried.

"Relax, close my eyes and let the dreams of fields and the river take over." She took a slow, peaceful breath and felt her body begin to unwind.

Carly woke and stared at the darkened room. "Darn it, I shouldn't have gone to sleep, now I missed her."

Angry with herself she decided to go down and make some tea. The house was quiet, Carly knew she would miss this place and more the people in the house.

Just as she finished pouring the hot water into the cup, she heard soft footsteps behind her. "Would you like a cup, Ruby?"

"Hmm, sounds good. Something must be bothering you to be up this late."

"I wish I woke earlier, I have a lot to tell you and more."

The lady smiled at her as if she already knew what Carly needed to say. "Sounds like a good time to talk."

They sat together at the table and Carly began to tell Ruby about the letters and what they contained. She didn't leave anything out and knew Ruby had many questions.

"Okay, that is the last that I know."

"My, this is all news to me. I do not think anyone knew that she and Mr. Glick were related."

"I didn't think so, either."

"Sounds like the lady lived in fear and that is not how we should be."

"No. It is sad that her cousin arrived too late to help her."

"I agree. What else is on your mind Carly, I've come to know your looks." Ruby smiled at her friend. "I will miss your company."

"You may think I am crazy about this, but here goes. I think you and I should go to the Bishop's house and check the basement. If the girls saw him kill the teacher, they could very well be there. Okay, that is it, and I need you to help me plan this."

Ruby stared at her and didn't speak, Carly felt sure the woman would no longer want her to be a friend.

"Me? Am I going to help you? Why not your friend Asher? Won't I be in the way?"

Ruby's questions flew through the air at a rapid staccato, not giving Carly any time to answer.

"Because Ruby, you know the area and I don't, and the girls know you not me."

"*Ach*, that is understandable. You know you'll have to tell me everything to do. I am not a detective." She laughed and pulled at the strings of her cap, a nervous habit.

Carly took a deep breath and smiled. Ruby could be such a hoot at times.

"Okay Ruby, how and when do we get into the Bishop's house?"

"You ask an easy question, my friend. Tomorrow is church Sunday. The Bishop will arrive at the Eischler's about eight o'clock. He and the ministers meet and pray about the service for an hour before the beginning. Then the service lasts for three hours. We can go across the fields to the Bishop's home after he leaves."

"Wasn't your last service at the Eischler's? I thought it was at a different home each time."

Ruby nodded. "It will be there because all that has gone on, no one has prepared their home. Mrs. Eischler has too much food, so it stands to reason all is ready there for Sunday."

Carly nodded. Would she ever grasp the Amish ways? "So, will you help me, Ruby? Won't someone see us?"

"*Nee*, everyone will be heading to church, but possibly we should wait until the service starts to be sure they are all there."

"They will miss you at the service, Ruby. We can't have the Bishop suspect we are up to anything."

Ruby ran her hand over the table's wood grain and pondered the dilemma. Finally, after some thought, she looked up into Carly's eyes. "I'll go to the service. Then before it starts, I'll feign illness. Asparagus makes me sick to my stomach. I'll nibble on some as I walk. By the time everyone is there, I'll go around the corner and start throwing up. Do you think that will work?" Ruby laughed at her scheme.

Carly joined her and giggled. "I can walk up the hill, so you don't have to double all the way back."

"Oh! Should we meet where we found poor Thomas Glick? We can see the bishop's *haus* from there." She got up and went for the hot teapot and returned to fill their cups. "We will know when he's gone."

"That sounds good, we can leave together, and I'll wait for you down by the creek it's a little closer to the road we have to cross."

"No one should be able to see you there. Especially Bishop Yoder. How can someone chosen by *Gott* become so evil?"

"People make their own evil, Ruby. It usually, starts with greed."

She stirred sugar into her cup before commenting. "I think the bishop is hungry for power over all the people in our district. He's overly stern and has shunned so many of our friends. The community has dwindled since he was chosen as bishop. Power and more power. Like he is *Gott*."

"I think you are right." Carly caught the sun's light in the window. "It is dawn already. No sense going to bed now."

"Carly, are you going to tell Asher our plans?"

Flashes of the other lost child gripped her, "No!"

"You look really upset. What happened? Of course, you don't have to tell me, but your reaction just now said many words." Ruby looked down to her lap, and she picked at a little spot of lint on the soft fabric of her nightgown.

Carly opened her mouth then closed it, "Now is not the time for past follies. We need all our concentration on the girls."

Ruby reached her hands across the table and took Carly's in hers. "Will you pray silently with me? I want to ask *Gott* to help us find the girls and if Bishop Yoder is guilty of taking them, bring him to justice."

"Yes, Ruby, I will call Asher the minute we know the girls are there."

Chapter 16

R uby came into the kitchen and found Carly pacing back and forth. "*Gute mariye*, Carly. Are you ready for our big day? I have a feeling we are going to find the girls. Hopefully, they are well after two weeks held captive."

"I know the girls are there, I can feel it. Those children better not be harmed, or the bishop may not make it out of the barn." Carly tried to smooth out her dark jeans forgetting she didn't have a skirt on.

"If the Bishop is guilty, what will happen to him? Our Amish district usually handles everything ourselves by shunning."

"I think your district can handle him with your laws, but he will be taken to jail and be charged for the dual kidnapping and most likely the murder of his wife and Thomas Glick. Once I call Asher, he will take over."

"Do you actually think he killed his wife, Carly?" Ruby sighed dejectedly.

"I am afraid he did. His wife's body will have to be exhumed to prove how she died, but regardless, he did kill Mr. Glick."

Ruby shuddered at the thought of exhumation.

"It's time for me to go with Matthew to the Eischler's. It's not far from here so I should have enough time to nibble my deadly vegetable." She laughed as she walked to the gas-powered refrigerator. Opening the door, she fussed around in the cold air and came out with a long piece.

Carly looked at her and said, "Don't make yourself so sick you can't go with me." Concern filled her eyes. "Oh, don't let Matthew see you nibbling that stalk."

"*Ach,* that would be a mishap. He's always reminding me to stop buying the vegetable, but my guests love my recipe for asparagus au gratin."

"I will vouch for that, it is delicious."

Matthew poked his head into the mudroom. "*Maem*, are you ready to go?" Seeing Carly in her jeans, he commented, "I see you aren't going with us today. You must be getting ready to leave tomorrow."

"I'm ready, and *jah*, Carly will be leaving." Ruby took a couple steps toward Carly and drew her into a hug. Whispering in her ear, she said, "See you in about thirty minutes. Be careful."

Carly smiled and gave her a slight nod. She watched them scoot out the back door and start their walk to service. She wouldn't leave for another twenty minutes or so, hoping that any passing buggies would be by this area before she started walking.

Unable to stand the confines of the kitchen, Carly headed for the porch and took her seat on the stairs. "Please, God make this all go well."

Carly couldn't sit still another moment, it should be clear to go. A smile came to her as she thought of the river and the day with Asher there, "it was special."

She almost thought of calling him with all this but refrained. He was a cop first, always. "And he couldn't help but do what he needed to for the case."

As she topped the rise, Carly heard something and quickly ducked into the corn stalks and kneeled just as a buggy sped past. She finally let out her breath and stood up. "That was too close."

Carly caught a glimpse of David and his children in the buggy. She knew he would have immediately stopped if he saw her, thankful he didn't.

By the time she made it down the hill to the creek, she needed a drink. She squatted down and dipped her cupped hands into the rushing water. The creek water was crystal clear and icy cool. "I needed that."

She found a nice shady spot under a tree and sat down to wait for Ruby. "You did surprise me, Ruby. There is a spark of adventure lit inside of you that you can't deny." Carly laughed to herself over the truth of it. She couldn't help but wonder what Ruby might be like outside of the Amish world.

Ruby's legs felt heavy as she and Matthew began their walk to the Eischler's. The asparagus felt heavy as a stone in her apron pocket, and she snapped a piece then slowly drew her hand out of the pocket. Feigning a cough, she slipped the portion into her mouth.

"Are you ok, *Maem*?" Matthew asked. "You look a little peaked today."

"I didn't sleep very well last night. I've been fretting about the missing girls. You know it's been two weeks today since they disappeared."

"*Jah,* you don't have to tell me. I miss Hannah so much. If she ever returns, I'm going to ask her to marry me."

Ruby looked at Matthew and smiled. "Not our traditional time of courtship, son."

He shook his head. "*Nee*, but if she shows up, that is exactly what I'm going to do. The Bishop be damned!"

"Matthew!" Ruby cried in shock, but deep down she approved. Bless her son and Hannah. Ruby limped as a rock flew into the side of her black tennis shoe. She bent down to take out the stone and slipped the last of the asparagus in her mouth. The Eischler's *haus* was in sight now. She just hoped she wouldn't vomit before arriving here.

"Remember Matthew you're only eighteen and Hannah is but seventeen."

Matthew laughed a bit. "The ages you and my father married?"

Her stomach churned, and she groaned.

"*Maem*, you *are* ill. Let me go borrow a buggy and take you home."

"*Nee*, I'm fine. Once we get into the barn for the service, it will be cooler in there, and I'll feel better."

She hadn't planned for this turn of events. Ruby should have known that Matthew would want to take care of her.

As they arrived at the barn, they were greeted by their friends from around the district. Her friend Martha rushed up to her, concern on her face. "Ruby you look terrible. Should you even be here?"

"Just a lack of sle—" her stomach took that moment to squeeze, and Ruby bent over and threw up on her friend's shoes.

"Dear *Gott*!" Martha cried. "Matthew come. Your *maem* is ill."

Martha's husband gripped her arm and pulled her away from Ruby and out of the mess between the friends. "Matthew, take the buggy and get your mother home before..."

Just as he said that Ruby took that moment to become ill again. She didn't remember the asparagus making her this sick. Shaking, her legs dropped her to the ground.

Just as Matthew was helping her up, someone came with a buggy. She wasn't sure whose it was, but she was ready to get out of the group of people. As she turned, she saw Bishop Yoder standing with his hands on his hips and shaking his head.

She looked up and saw David Fisher in his buggy with the twins. "Matthew, take the children. I'll take your mother home."

Matthew nodded and helped the children out of the buggy and found David beside her.

David picked up Ruby and sat her on the seat.

Ruby felt her eyes go wide and a sudden shiver roll through her body. This wasn't a reaction from the asparagus, it was from the closeness of David Fisher. Her emotions were now all mixed up with nausea and excitement. Now wasn't the time for her body to become interested in the opposite sex!

The buggy swayed back and forth causing nausea to gain the upper hand as they traversed the dirt road. Suddenly Ruby leaned over and told David to stop. She heaved over the side of the buggy. Hopefully, this was the last of it. There was no way she could help Carly as sick as she was.

About a quarter of a mile later, she snapped, "Stop David."

Immediately, he pulled the reins on the horse, and they stopped in the middle of the road. When Ruby didn't lean over the side of the buggy, he asked, "Are you ok? What is the problem?"

"The next road to the left, turn there."

"Why?"

"Don't ask. You'll see in just a little bit. We are going to meet Carly at the back road."

David shook his head and snapped the reins and turned down the path leading to the creek.

"What the heck?" Carly stood up and watched as the buggy started down the dirt path. She sucked in her breath and waited in the dark shadow to see who was coming. Eventually, she could tell, "Ruby what have you done?"

She started walking up to the slowing buggy not sure what to say or do, but she would refuse not to go inside the bishop's house.

As the buggy came to a halt, David jumped down and tipped his hat to her before going around the other side to help Ruby down.

If her friend didn't look so darn sick, she would be yelling at her. Carly didn't have to ask what happened, "too much asparagus, Ruby?"

"*Jah* and David offered to take me home. For as sick as I am, I thought it would be good to have him along. I'm too—" Again she heaved, but nothing came out. She was empty. Moaning, she dropped to the ground. "You tell him what you need to, Carly. I have to lie back on the grass and close my eyes for just a moment."

Carly looked at David and just stared at him for a moment. When he would have talked, she spoke up. "David, I think your daughter and Mary are being kept in the Bishop's basement. Ruby and I were going to break in and see if we could find them..."

David didn't wait for her to say more, he took hold of her elbow and said, "let's go now."

"Okay." Carly looked back at Ruby and saw the woman wave her off.

"Why asparagus?"

"Oh, well they make her sick." Carly tried to smile but failed, "I think she ate too much of it."

"No kidding," they heard Ruby say from the ground.

David grunted and shook his head. "You two women can be quite a handful." He flicked the reins and off they went.

"There is a small bridge to your right," Ruby cried out to them, and she fell back into the grass."

David laughed.

"This is serious!" Carly snapped.

"*Jah*, but funny as well. This story needs to be shown in the live performance they have yearly at the annex to the eatery on the main street." Again, the sound of his laughter came across Carly's nerves.

Within minutes they were at the bishop's house. No one was around, and the air was suddenly quiet.

David thought if Hannah were around here somewhere, she would be screaming for help. Unless she thought the bishop had come back.

He reined in the horses then hopped out. Before he could go around the back of the buggy to help Carly out, she was already at his side.

"Let's try the front door, David, I doubt if he locks it, he is too cocky."

He raced up the steps and twisted the knob. "Unlocked."

Carly raced into the house trying any door that looked like it might be the basement. And then, she saw it, a padlock on the door. David was right behind her.

"Damn him."

"Can you open it, David?"

He rushed out the kitchen door and into the living room. He spotted a poker near the firebox and grabbed it. He ran back into the kitchen. "Get out of the way, Carly!" He stabbed the poker into the door crack, shoving until the small end easily sank into the slot.

"Hannah! Mary! It's *daed*! I'm coming for you."

With a will of determination, he reared back on the poker, and as he did so, the door popped open taking the padlock with it. Before him was a hole filled with darkness. His eyes adjusted quickly, and he saw the stairs.

Carly didn't try to get past David this was his daughter, and she prayed to *Gott* that the girls were alright.

David raced down the stairs, reached out his hand to pull the light cord that had slapped him in the face as he reached the bottom step. The light glowed, and he saw both Hannah and Mary. They were tied to a post near the corner of the room. "Carly find a knife and bring it here, quickly! The girls are tied up down here."

Carly didn't hesitate, she ran up the stairs and straight to the kitchen where she pulled a large butcher knife out of the block.

Nearly falling off the last steps, she rushed to David and handed him the knife. She watched as he carefully freed Mary and then Hannah who fell into his waiting arms. Carly moved over to Mary and helped her stand, her legs were weak, and she nearly carried her. "David they can't walk, too weak."

Suddenly, they heard the sound of wheels and the neighing of a horse. "Shhh…" David started. "Who can that be?"

"The bishop!" Hannah cried and dropped back to the floor as she sobbed. "He's going to catch all of us and kill us like he bragged to us about killing his wife and Mr. Glick! We saw him kill the *mann*, we didn't know it was Mr. Glick until he said so. He saw us and caught us because we were too scared to move."

Both the girls held each other, and David motioned for them to be quiet. He slowly made his way up the cement steps leading to the kitchen. As he looked out, he gasped. "Asher! What are you doing here? In a buggy?"

"I could ask the same question, looks like you beat me to it. I took a buggy and a horse from my *daed's,* so I wouldn't raise anyone's suspicions." Asher looked over David's shoulder and saw Carly hugging the girls. "Yeah, I should have known you'd be here."

"She found them, Asher." David cleared his throat, "Can you carry Mary up and I'll get Hannah? Carly is right, they are too weak to walk."

"Will do. Is the bishop at service?"

"He better be."

Asher didn't need to say more...

Asparagus au Gratin

Ingredients
    1/4 cup unsalted butter
1/4 cup all-purpose flour
1 3/4 cups chicken broth
1/4 cup light cream
3/4 cup grated Cheddar cheese
1/2 cup Parmesan cheese
salt and pepper
36 asparagus spears
Instructions
Cook asparagus in a large pot of boiling, salted water until just barely tender. Strain and set aside.

In a saucepan, melt the butter, add the flour and stir with a wire whisk until well blended. Meanwhile, bring the chicken broth and cream to a boil and add all at once to a butter-flour mixture, stirring vigorously with the whisk until the sauce is thickened and smooth. Add the cheeses, salt, and pepper, and stir until cheeses melt.

Place alternate layers of sauce and asparagus in a buttered casserole, ending with a layer of sauce. Sprinkle with additional Parmesan cheese and brown quickly under a preheated broiler or bake in preheated oven at 450 degrees for 5 minutes.

Chapter 17

Carly caught herself as the buggy dipped to the right then left. The silence between her and Asher felt deafening. She didn't have to look at him to know he was livid with her and all she wanted to do was laugh.

When Asher saw Ruby lying on the ground, he lost it thinking she was another victim of the bishop. Even Ruby laughed through her groans. Carly swore that lady would never touch another asparagus.

But not Asher, no he didn't even crack a smile. Carly told herself she would be lucky not to be thrown in the cell beside the Bishop.

Ruby called out to them, "The girls, did you find the girls?" She dropped back on the grass, weakness filled her.

"Asher help me get Ruby in the buggy, and I'll get into the back."

At least, he got out of the buggy. Carly saw Ruby raise her eyebrows in question.

"Yes, they were there as we thought. They are in the buggy with David."

"Come on Ruby, let's get you in the buggy and catch up with David. He promised he wouldn't go in until we were there with them at the service, I already called for an ambulance and the crime scene investigators. That man is going away for a very long time."

Asher put Ruby gently into the buggy and helped Carly maneuver to the back. He wanted to scream at her, spank her, anything! She took too significant a risk on this one. But he couldn't, and he'd rather kiss her for being alive.

Ruby groaned from beside him. "Asher. I can't tell if you want to kill Carly or tell her that you love her. I think the latter would be the best."

The man just sort of growled at Ruby and Carly managed to swallow her laughter.

Asher sighed, they managed to pull in, right behind David's buggy. "Ladies, shall we go get him."

"We should before David gets his hands on the *mann*."

Ruby said under her breath.

He helped both ladies out of the buggy and followed them over to David to help with the girls. Asher went to David's side, "Let me handle this David, I need to read him his rights and get the cuffs on him."

"It would be best, though I have feelings much more dangerous."

Asher gripped the man's shoulder, "I understand. Take care of Hannah and Mary. I don't think they can walk yet."

Asher watched to make sure David went to the girls. He could imagine what the man had gone through these last weeks. The bishop would deserve everything he gets.

He moved forward into the barn and stopped a moment to let his eyes adjust to the different lighting. Once he could see he stepped forward toward the Bishop. He waited for the man to acknowledge his presence and the Bishop saw him and did precisely what Asher expected.

The Bishop raised his fist and glared at Asher. "Get out you heathen, get out you are shunned from our sight!"

Asher caught sight of his mother rising from the bench, he raised his hand for her to stay put and she did. He didn't bother looking for his father.

"Mr. Eischler and Mr. King remove this *mann* from our service. NOW!"

The Bishop was still ranting at him to the point that spittle flew out with his anger. "Sit down Bishop, and that is an order."

Asher turned to the men, "Mr. Eischler please go outside," Asher looked over to Mrs. Eischler, "Mrs. Eischler, please go out as well and join Mr. Fisher. Matthew, I want you to go as well, your mother is out there, please." He waited for them to leave the building before turning back to the fuming man behind him. "The rest of you, please stay, I think you all need to find out what kind of man is leading this district."

He looked around ready to stare down anyone that moved, this would be done his way. Turning to the Bishop, who of course didn't follow his order. "I am arresting you, Eli Yoder for the murder of your wife Naomi and Mr. Thomas Glick, also for the kidnapping of Hannah Fisher and Mary Eischler. You have the right..." Asher pulled out his handcuffs to force the man to his knees and put them on behind his back as he read him his rights. When he finished, he pulled him up to stand in front of the barn full of worshipers.

The congregation gasped then the women began crying. Their husbands stood and hollered at Asher. They demanded an explanation.

The Bishop screamed in his face, "I will have your job for this."

Asher ignored the man, he stayed quiet as the Fishers and Eischler's entered the barn to stand beside him. Each father held their daughter in his arms as they were too weak to stand. "I will also add to these charges torture and negligence."

David moved Hannah from his arms and sat her on a bench by the barn door by Matthew and Ruby, then walked between the seats to the pulpit. "Everyone settle down. I have information, but it can't be disclosed just yet. We must wait for the police to conclude their investigation, but bishop Yoder held our daughters hogtied in his basement. As you can see, they are now free."

The congregation turned their heads to look at the girls. Their words flew from them, but the consensus was, they were shocked, but thrilled the girls had been found.

Sirens pierced the early morning air. Asher knew that would be the ambulance and the squad arriving. Vehicle doors slammed, and the EMTs arrived with two gurneys for the girls. Gently they placed the victims on the gurneys and began their vital intake.

Asher spoke once again. "I think this service has ended for the day, everyone. Why don't you disband with a prayer and then get your refreshments at the house and backyard? We've had enough excitement for one day."

At that, the EMTs wheeled the girls to the ambulance, and the police officers had Mr. Yoder locked in the back of a squad car.

Asher went to the officers and told them to take the bishop directly to Lancaster where he would be booked. "I'll be along as soon as I get this mess cleared up. I notified the CSIs, and they are on the way to the Yoder house. The whole farm is a crime scene. It may take a while to process."

Someone placed a plastic cup in his hand. He looked up and saw Carly standing by his side. "Thank you. I really needed this." As he took a sip, he saw his parents coming out the barn door and head toward him.

"I'll catch you in a bit, Carly. We have a lot to talk about." Asher turned on his heel and met his parents.

"*Maem, Daed*...I'm sorry you had to witness this. Father, I know you trusted the Bishop, but he didn't deserve it." His father looked down at the ground for a bit, then raised his eyes and looked directly into his son's. "Your mother has been right all along, hasn't she?"

Ash nodded in response. "I'm sorry as well, *Daed*. I've missed my family since this shunning, but I can't come home as an Amish man. I hope you'll both understand."

His father grabbed him in a hug. "I've missed you as well. We shall welcome you home and back into our lives. This Bishop caused the divide, and we can now see how awful his actions have been for our district."

"Come home when you finish up this work," His mother interjected. I have your favorite pie made. Strawberry rhubarb."

Asher smiled and hugged his mother as well. "Plan on it, *Maem*. I'm not sure of the time, but I'll be there. I've missed you all so much."

They all went their separate ways, and Asher went to find Carly.

Chapter 18

Ruby looked out the kitchen window and saw Carly sitting by herself on the swing hanging from the tall oak tree in the side yard. She felt so sorry for the woman. Here she planned to have a nice break and gain her emotional strength from the horrible case she had over the past few months. A thought struck Ruby. She dried her hands, and then went outside to talk to her new friend.

Walking up to the silent woman she spoke softly, "Carly, can I speak to you for a moment. I hope I'm not intruding on your thoughts."

"No problem, Ruby. I am just waiting for Asher to come by. He said he would be over."

"Do you think he's still livid about our interference in the bishop's case?" Ruby grasped the tightly wound rope attached to a tire beside the swing where Carly sat. She placed herself in the tire for a place to relax.

"He was furious at me, I could see it, he wanted to yell but held back because his parents were there." Carly took a deep breath and push off the swing.

Ruby followed her lead. In a moment, they were both swinging high in the air and giggling like a couple ten-year-olds.

"Ruby? Did you hear something?" Before Carly could say more a voice, she knew very well spoke up before he pushed her swing. "Asher."

"Yeah, it must be nice to be so carefree with all that has happened."

Both the ladies stopped swinging and got off the swings to turn and look at him.

Ruby took Carly's hand. "I'll let you two talk, but before I do, I'd like to invite you, Carly, to stay another two weeks. Your vacation was disrupted helping our district solve this mystery of the missing girls then Thomas Glick's death. You deserve a nice long rest. Free of charge."

Carly didn't hesitate to reach out and hug her friend. "I would love to stay, you need to teach me how to make those pies."

"Thank you. I'm so glad you'll stay. I'd miss having you around. Now, I have food to make. I invited David and his family, the Eischler's and I'd love to have you, Asher, come for supper at seven. I already reached your parents and they are coming. We all need to talk about what has happened. *Denbriefing* is what you call it?"

"It is called debriefing, Ruby and yes I would like to come to dinner, thank you."

"I'll come in and help you." Carly turned to follow her.

"Hold on a minute there missy. We have a lot to talk about."

Carly could hear the firmness in his voice and really wanted to walk away, but it wouldn't be right not to hear him out. "Ruby, I will be in as soon as Asher, and I are done."

Carly turned and started up the slight incline to the porch, she could hear Asher's impatient footsteps behind her. She wondered what he would do if she started running, she grinned, deciding not to try it.

She took a seat on the top step and faced Asher. "Okay, I am here."

"Why didn't you call me, Carly?"

"I was going to, but you showed up just as we got the girls freed."

"You do know I could charge you with interfering with the case."

"You could, I guess."

He gave a defeated smile and slowly shook his head. "Why the Bishop?"

"The letter, it all pointed to him."

"I am glad you found them, they are in terrible shape. The girls said the bishop rarely fed them and then just scraps."

"The man is a monster. Did they tell you he admitted to killing both his wife and her cousin?"

"Yes, Hannah told me. I will get a more thorough statement once she is rested. Poor Mary is in worse shape, she said he hit her a couple times and for no reason."

"Damn him, what makes someone so cruel?"

"I think, the Bishop was finished, and he knew it. I don't think the girls had much time left. We found two graves dug up in the lower field. You saved their lives, Carly."

"We all did. I am just glad it is over." She smiled at him. "Do you think there will be a trial?"

"That will depend on how he pleas at the arraignment."

"He is so pompous that he will probably demand a trial." Carly wanted to spit, and Asher grinned at her knowing she wouldn't.

"Carly, I need to go to the station. Tell Ruby for me that I will try very hard to be on time, but I might be late."

"We will put up a plate for you for when you arrive."

Before Ash turned to leave, he stopped and looking at her, "Carly, I wanted to tell you that I took the Captain's job at Paradise Wells. I think it will be a good move."

"That is wonderful for you Asher, I am so happy for you."

"Yeah, it will be a good move, I am going to take this weekend to find someplace to live."

"Do you want some company?"

"You know I would, we can decide on a time for me to pick you up later tonight."

"Sounds good, congratulations."

"Thank you."

Carly watched him walk up the road, she called out, "It's closer to home."

Asher waved, and she could hear his laughter carry on the wind.

Chapter 19

Ruby pulled the pot roast from the oven. It was covered with sliced onion, carrot coins, and potato halves. Most of the meal was in this one large roaster. She had dinner rolls from the freezer defrosted. They only needed a warmup in the oven. Banana pies lined the countertops.

Matthew returned from the hospital. He poked his head in and told her that Hannah and Mary were doing better. The doctors were giving them fluids by IV and feeding them easy to digest foods. If all went well, they could come home in a couple days.

"That is a lot of food, *Maem*," he said as his eyes grew round as he looked at her offerings.

"I invited the Eischlers', Fishers', and Asher's family for supper. We need to unwind."

"A good one as well," Matthew said. "I knew the Bishop was rigid, but I would never have supposed he was a murdering kidnapper." He shook his head. "I'll go shower and be back over in a bit. Before I do, is there any way I can help you?"

"*Nee,* I am nearly finished. You just get ready and come back when you can."

Matthew gave her a hug, then turned and left the kitchen for his home in the small house near the main residence.

Ruby and Carly finally sat down once the meal preparation and setting the table was completed. Asher's parents smiled at the women and took a seat as well. Carly thanked God the girls were safe and the man responsible was in jail. At least the old bishop wouldn't be out anytime soon with the murders he was also guilty of committing.

The thought made her smile to herself, *I came here to relax and get away from all this and here I sit in the middle of mayhem.* Yet, there were many good things that came with the troubles these last few weeks. She gained a new friend, Ruby, the lady of the house and her son Matthew. Both were rather progressive in dealing with the Englisch.

Carly thought about Asher a lot these last couple of weeks. Before coming here their relationship dissolved in a lot of bitterness. She thought it was totally over. Now, well they would see. At least he restored his relationship with his parents after years of being shunned by the Amish. Another of the bishop's many disasters to be repaired and maybe for more than just Asher.

She felt happy for Asher. He told her he took the captain's job in Paradise Wells and would be moving there. It was closer to his parents and she figured that had a lot to do with his decision. She would be looking forward to helping him find a place to live for his new job.

David, Asher, Matthew, and the Eischler's entered the kitchen together. Everyone already at the table grew silent. They all wanted the newest update on the girls and their condition in the hospital. Carly caught the slight nod David gave Matthew to proceed. Ruby's son stood there looking at everyone, he looked so much older to her, but much happier. The poor girls were weak and malnourished, they probably wouldn't be leaving the hospital for a few days,

"But they are doing much better," David offered.

"Thanks to *Gott*!" Mr. Eischler exclaimed. "It's too bad that our lives will not go back to normal for quite a while. What is going to happen to the Bishop, Asher?"

"He's been charged with kidnapping your girls, and with the death of Thomas Glick and his wife. They still have to exhume her body,"

Asher said as he pulled out a chair. He motioned for the Eischler's to sit by him.

After the silent prayer, Ruby began the meal and took a serving of meat and a few carrots. "What is going to happen to our *Ordnung* and church without a Bishop?" Ruby asked.

Mr. Eischler spoke up. "Some of the community members checked with the bishop in the next district. They were told the longest-serving minister should take over until we can draw from the lot. Then the newly selected bishop will take on the duties."

Asher's father joined the conversation, "We need to review all the shunning cases that the *mann* instigated. I know for a fact that many should never have happened and that includes my son."

"From your mouth to God's ear," Asher said and brought the gathering to tearful laughter and relief.

THE END

Did you love *In Plain Sight*? Then you should read *Amish Heritage*[1] by Piper Forrest and Lily Simmons!

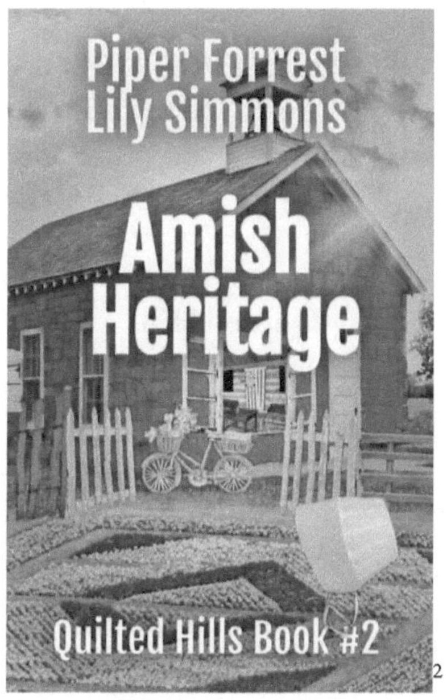

[2]

Book 2 of the Quilted Hills Series

Some say Paradise Wells' Amish are too progressive. Cell phones, selling online, and yet, they are steeped in historical lore.

Newlywed healer--a Braucherei, and midwife, **Miriam Miller** and her husband, **Levi** struggle with her healing activities in the community. Levi finds he is better with his horses than his wife's unpredictable schedule.

Amid stolen horses, births, and healings will their love conquer all?

---

1. https://books2read.com/u/4DEoaD

2. https://books2read.com/u/4DEoaD

Also by Piper Forrest

Quilted Hills
In Plain Sight
Amish Heritage
One Amish Autumn
My Amish Rose
Amish At Heart

Also by Lily Simmons

Quilted Hills
In Plain Sight
Amish Heritage
One Amish Autumn
My Amish Rose
Amish At Heart